P9-ARM-383

South Shore Billionaires

Billionaires finding brides!

Bonded at boarding school, best friends Jeremy, Branson and Cole have scaled the world's rich lists and become New York's wealthiest tycoons.

Now these billionaires are swapping the bright lights of the city for the blue waters and golden sands of the coast. In stunning South Shore, they'll find love and taste a life they never knew they wanted!

Read Jeremy's story in

Christmas Baby for the Billionaire

And look out for Branson's and Cole's stories

Coming soon!

Dear Reader,

Welcome to a new trilogy—the South Shore Billionaires! I had so much fun writing this holiday story to kick it off. There are so many of my personal loves in this book, from favorite holiday movies to the scent of evergreens to Junior's pineapple cheesecake—introduced to me by Damon Suede and which I agreed was "life changing." Christmas in New York is magical!

I wrote this story during a time when I was facing a lot of emotional challenges. It's funny how life sometimes sends you multiple crises in a row and somehow you get through it. It's pretty appropriate, then, that the beach by the Sandpiper Resort is based on a place my husband and I visit each summer; a stunning, kilometer-long stretch of sand on Nova Scotia's South Shore. Why is it appropriate? Because as I was dealing with each crisis, my husband was right there with me, holding my hand and being my rock. Just like he has been for the past twenty-three years. (Yes, clearly I was a child bride!)

I hope you get swept away in Jeremy and Tori's story! And look for Bran's story, coming soon!

With love,

Donna

Christmas Baby for the Billionaire

Donna Alward

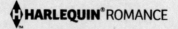

HARLEQUIN® ROMANCE

Recycling programs
for this product may
not exist in your area.

ISBN-13: 978-1-335-49956-1

Christmas Baby for the Billionaire

First North American publication 2019

Copyright © 2019 by Donna Alward

Printed in U.S.A.

Donna Alward lives on Canada's east coast with her family, which includes her husband, a couple of kids, a senior dog and two crazy cats. Her heartwarming stories of love, hope and homecoming have been translated into several languages, hit bestseller lists and won awards, but her favorite thing is hearing from readers! When she's not writing, she enjoys reading (of course), knitting, gardening, cooking...and she is a *Masterpiece* addict. You can visit her on the web at donnaalward.com and join her mailing list at donnaalward.com/newsletter.

Books by Donna Alward

Harlequin Romance

Destination Brides

Summer Escape with the Tycoon

Marrying a Millionaire

Best Man for the Wedding Planner
Secret Millionaire for the Surrogate

Holiday Miracles

Sleigh Ride with the Rancher

Heart to Heart

Hired: The Italian's Bride

Visit the Author Profile page
at Harlequin.com for more titles.

To Mum. The older I get, the more I admire your strength and your capacity for unconditional love. Your children and grandchildren have been incredibly blessed.

CHAPTER ONE

THERE WERE MORNINGS when a girl just didn't want to get out of bed, but she had to because a) she had to pee and b) she had to go to work because no one else was going to pay the bills.

Tori closed her eyes, gathered her get-up-and-go and threw off the covers. It wasn't that she didn't like her job; she loved it. The Sandpiper Resort was her life. She'd started there doing housekeeping as a teenager and had worked her way up to assistant general manager, overseeing many of the day-to-day operations. Stepping inside the doors each morning felt as much like being at home as entering her own small house, bought just last year.

So even though she was bone tired, despite having slept all night, she flipped on the light switch and turned on the shower. At least the morning sickness had been fleeting, lasting only a few weeks and consisting mostly of inconvenient nausea. Now in her second trimester, she simply got tired more easily. And was in the process of overhauling her wardrobe. Things didn't fit anymore now that her baby bump had made an appearance.

Thirty minutes later, hair blow-dried and makeup on, she left the house with her decaf coffee in a travel mug and made the five-minute drive to work. It had been mild for November, and she didn't have to scrape the frost off her windshield this morning, which was a plus. On arriving at the hotel, she stepped inside, inhaling the fresh scent of evergreens. Once Remembrance Day had passed, the Christmas decorations had come out, turning the resort into a fairyland of white twinkle lights and pungent pine and spruce boughs punctuated with gorgeous red and gold bows. She greeted the staff at the front desk with a smile, then stopped at the kitchen to ask for a toasted bagel and some fruit—her usual breakfast fare.

"You need some eggs for the little one, there?" Neil asked, his chef's hat bobbing. "Mamas need protein."

She grinned. "When are you gonna stop pampering me?" she asked, taking a sip of her coffee. For a few weeks, she'd been turned off the smell of the brew. Now she inhaled the richness of it and sighed.

"Never," he replied, his eyes crinkling at the corners. Neil had been working in this kitchen since before she'd started cleaning rooms. Pretty soon his granddaughter would be looking for a summer job.

Eggs did sound good this morning, so she smiled. "You know how I like them," she acquiesced. "Thanks, Neil. You're a gem."

"You betcha."

Ten minutes later one of the waitstaff brought her breakfast, as well as a glass of milk. "Neil says you need your calcium," Ellen said, and even though she was younger than Tori, her voice came across as motherly.

"Neil is being overprotective and I love it," she remarked, smiling up at the waitress who'd joined their team last May. "Thanks." She unrolled her cutlery from the napkin. "Everything going okay in the dining room?"

Ellen nodded. "Slower now that the leaves are gone and no one really comes for the beach."

"I know. I'm sorry about the cut hours."

"It's okay. It's a seasonal thing. We all get it."

"We've got some holiday events planned, so if you're up for working those, I'll make sure you're on the list for scheduling." The ticketed events always meant decent tips, and Ellen's eyes lit up.

"I'd appreciate that. Thanks, Tori."

"No problem. It helps a bit when regular hours are short and Christmas is coming." Besides, Ellen had proved herself to be competent and reliable. Throwing a few extra hours her way was small reward.

Once Ellen was gone, Tori dug into her breakfast. Neil had added cheese to her eggs, and a little parsley...delicious. There were two slices of honeydew and a little dish of fresh strawberries, plus a whole-grain bagel with her favorite topping—plain cream cheese sprinkled with cinnamon sugar.

They really were a family around here, taking care of each other. Which was good for Tori, because it was only her and her mom now. Her mom, Shelley, was a nurse and had taken a job at the hospital in Lunenburg. It wasn't far away, but after Tori's father had died of cancer, Shelley had moved into an apartment right in the town for convenience. It put her about fifty kilometers away—close enough for weekly visits.

Tori put her hand on the swell of her belly. Now she was going to have her own family. And she *was* happy, deep down. The question of whether or not to have the baby hadn't even been brought up. She didn't have much family, and now she'd have a baby to love, and he or she would love her in return. Her mother would have a grandchild. Circumstances weren't ideal, but Tori had started thinking of this pregnancy as a surprise blessing.

The bagel caught in her throat and she took a deep drink of the milk to wash it down along with the unease that kept nagging her when she thought of her decision not to tell the father—at least not yet. Every time she'd determined to say nothing, she heard her mother's voice telling her that Jeremy deserved to know. The problem was, she agreed with her mom. She wasn't going to be able to keep this from him forever. She just had to figure out the logistics. The right way.

Jeremy Fisher... What had she been thinking, getting caught up with him last summer? It had been two weeks of sheer bliss, during which time she'd completely lost her head. They'd agreed it was a holiday romance, and boy, had they made the most of their time together. When it was over, he'd gone back to his life in New York and she'd been left behind in small-town Nova Scotia, in a tiny house on the water. And that had been exactly as she'd wanted it. She wasn't a fairy-tale kind of woman, with dreams of being whisked away to a lavish lifestyle and a happy ever after. Well, she had been, once. She'd been swept off her feet by a handsome man with tons of plans. Riley had seemed perfect on the surface. And she'd fallen for him, hard.

Until she realized he'd been living a double life. He'd showered her with gifts and affection, but behind it all was a history of defrauding people and going into debt. For a long time she'd blamed herself for being so stupid.

She bit into a strawberry and considered her summer affair. Perhaps her "relationship" with Jeremy had been different because from the start there had been no question that it would be anything other than a fling. Indeed, it had been quite out of character for her, considering he was a guest at the resort. But they'd been discreet. And after two years of hard work, losing her dad and feeling alone, she'd given herself permission to enjoy this one thing.

She hadn't thought there'd be these kinds of consequences.

The power dynamic hadn't mattered during those few weeks. But it mattered now. Jeremy was a rich, powerful man, and she was...well, not *nobody*. She had enough self-esteem to give herself that much. But she certainly didn't have the same clout and resources at her disposal, and it made for a very uneven balance between them.

She shook her head and pushed her plate aside, eager to get to work. The hotel manager, Thomas, was on vacation this week, so it was up to Tori to steer the ship. She spent the morning at her desk, then met with the housekeeping manager and the catering manager about requirements for a holiday function scheduled for mid-December. There was a Christmas wedding planned for the weekend before the twenty-fifth, and another on New Year's Eve, where the ceremony would actually begin just before midnight so the bride and groom would be the first married couple of the new year. They were making a number of special accommodations for that event, from late checkout the next day to food service at one in the morning. The couple was willing to pay, so the hotel was willing to take their business.

It was mid-afternoon when she got up to do a walk-around, to get out of her office and to talk to staff and see what was happening. It was her favorite time of the day, actually, chatting with the staff, wandering through her second home, caring for it with love and affection. She made a note of a ding in a corner wall that would need to be touched up with paint, and gave a mental check mark to whoever had cleaned the public bathrooms on the lobby level. They sparkled and smelled like the hotel's custom lemongrass-and-ginger scent. She greeted staff by name and made a few more notes about additional Christmas decorations that could be added to the dining room and small on-site gift shop. Maybe business was slower this time of year, but for those who did arrive for an escape or a special dinner, the hotel would show to best advantage.

She was just returning to the administration offices when the front door blew open, bringing in a smattering of brown leaves and rain; a man was propelled in with them, shaking his arms to rid his coat of water droplets.

She turned to the sound…and froze.

"Tori?"

She'd never known that a person could feel blood rush out of their face, but she felt it now.

No.

No, no, no, no, no.

He couldn't be here. This was all wrong.

"Jeremy."

He grinned widely, his thousand-watt smile hitting her right in the solar plexus. Why did he have to be so handsome? "I hoped you'd be here. What's it been? Four months?"

Four months, three weeks, and five days, she wanted to answer, but nothing came out of her mouth. What was he doing here? And could she escape without him noticing the obvious?

No such luck. At her silence, his gaze swept down, then back up, and his eyes were filled with questions and confusion. Of course, she'd chosen today to unveil her new maternity wardrobe. Her *condition* was perfectly plain for all to see.

"Why don't you step into my office?" she asked, pulling herself together. "We can catch up. What brings you back to the Sandpiper?" Her voice came out smooth and steady, thankfully. It wouldn't do for him to see her discomposed.

She turned her back and started toward the offices, her body trembling. Not just because of the lie of omission he'd caught her in, but because just the sight of him still had the power to turn her knees to jelly.

It had been a very good few weeks, after all. Too good.

She heard his steps behind her and once they were in her office, she shut the door. Staff might be family, but they didn't need to hear every conversation, and no one here knew the identity of her baby's father. She and Jeremy had tried to be discreet.

Her office was small, and felt smaller still with him in it. She turned around and faced him, finally, attempting to put up an emotional wall so she could maintain her objectivity. It was harder than she'd imagined. Jeremy had a presence about him that was magnetic. Today he was dressed in a charcoal-gray suit with a precisely knotted tie, and an overcoat that protected him from the cold Atlantic wind. His hair was tousled, as though the ocean breeze had fingers it had run through the strands, making them seem carelessly styled, and tiny drops of rain sparkled on the top. And his eyes… Right now his eyes were the same steel gray as the white-capped waves along the shore. Cold and unhappy. Her tummy turned over with anxiety.

"What brings you back to the area?" she asked,

feigning a smile, skirting around him to sit behind her desk. Her tummy was hidden that way…

"Real estate. And I thought I'd look you up again while I was here. I didn't expect to find you pregnant."

The blunt statement hit her like a slap. So much for the hope of him not cluing in. It had been a long shot but she'd held out a smidgen of hope that her top might have camouflaged her bump.

She shrugged. "To be honest, it was a surprise to me, too."

"Is it mine?"

Her stomach plummeted. There was no beating around the bush with him. Never had been. Right from the start, he'd been up front about his attraction to her. He'd been staying in their best suite and she'd checked in on him on the first day to make sure everything was okay. They'd ended up chatting for a long time, about the area and about how different it was from his life in the Big Apple. When he'd invited her out for a drink she'd said yes, and it had been over a pomegranate martini that he'd told her she had the most intriguing eyes of anyone he'd ever met. She'd been charmed…and wooed.

She'd admired his confidence and honesty then, though she wasn't such a big fan of it at this moment.

For the briefest time, she considered saying

no. It would solve a lot. But that simple answer was complicated by the small matter of her conscience. She had already been struggling with the fact that she hadn't yet told him about the pregnancy. Then there was a certain amount of integrity at stake. There had been no one else. He'd been the only one.

"Of course it is. I don't…make a habit of what happened between us."

He regarded her dispassionately. "How was I to know that? And were you ever going to tell me?"

Curse her and her honesty. She held his gaze, determined not to cower. "Eventually. And thanks for that wonderful endorsement of my character. It's always pleasant to be shamed by your baby's father."

He let out a breath and turned away for a moment, before turning back again. His gray eyes were contrite. "I'm sorry. That was uncalled for. It's just… This is a hell of a surprise, Tori."

"Yes," she said, "I'm sure it is."

"When…how…?"

Tori picked up a pen and played with it, resolving to keep up her appearance of strength. "We both know the answer to that question. Early July, and presumably one of the times we had sex."

She did not call it making love, though it had certainly felt like that at the time. Her cheeks heated as a memory swept through her. As hokey as it sounded, she had a feeling that she knew exactly when it had happened. They'd spent the day at the beach, splashing about in the water and having a picnic on the sand. And then in the late afternoon they'd gone back to her place and had finished off the day by taking their sweet time with each other.

He'd been a fantastic lover. Gentle, attentive, passionate.

Now, with him standing in her office, at the very least unhappy and very likely angry, those sweet memories were somehow tarnished.

He let out a huge breath. "May I sit?"

She held out a hand. "Of course." She wasn't exactly in a position to deny him anything right now, was she? The fears she'd had about him knowing about the baby were all crammed into her brain and she fought hard to ignore them. Perhaps she could put him off somehow, so she could prepare what she wanted to say to him.

He pulled out the guest chair, then shrugged out of his coat and laid it over the back before sitting. He leaned forward onto his knees, resting on his elbows. Tori bit down on her lip. It wasn't fair that he was so handsome. His brown hair and strong chin were reminiscent of JFK Jr., to her mind, but instead of his eyes being a rich brown, they were gray and heavily lashed. And right now they were looking at her with something like accusation and disappointment in their depths.

"I'm going to be a father," he said, his voice rough. "You're halfway through your pregnancy… When were you going to tell me?"

Her hands shook so she folded them on top of her desk. "I don't know. I was waiting for the right time, and I've been going back and forth about it every day." She figured honesty was the best policy here; Jeremy would see through any attempt to mollify or placate him, and he'd definitely sense a lie.

His voice hardened. "I have a right to know."

This was the hard part. Just this morning she'd come to work like any other day. There was comfort in that. More than anything, Jeremy transported her out of her comfort zone and she struggled to find her feet in order to deal with this conversation.

She met his gaze again. "Our circumstances are a bit unique, you know. We had a fling. We live far apart, in two very different worlds. And I have no idea how to structure a co-parenting arrangement with someone who is, in many ways, a stranger." She took a breath. "You have resources I don't and I would lose in any sort of power struggle if you made a play for custody." There. She'd said it. No sense beating around the bush.

He sat back then, the questions in his eyes replaced by... Could it be? He was hurt by her last statement. Or at least offended. Her pulse was hammering so hard right now she couldn't quite trust her observations.

"Do you really think I'd do such a thing?"

She sat up straighter. "As I said, we don't really know each other, do we? It wasn't a chance I was willing to take. I'd die before letting someone take my baby away."

Jeremy tried to breathe through the cramping in his chest. He'd been looking forward to surprising Tori today. Work had brought him back to the area on behalf of a client and he'd imagined reigniting the flame that had raged between them last summer. Truthfully, he hadn't been able to get her out of his head, and this work trip on Branson's behalf had given him the perfect excuse to get her out of his system once and for all.

Instead he'd found her carrying his baby. The pregnancy shook him to the core, but the veiled accusation he'd just heard...that was a real gut punch.

He was a straight shooter and liked to think he was a good man. But right now he held back the words forming in his brain and those already stuck in his throat. Because he was confused, and angry, and another emotion he couldn't quite place. Hurt was part of it. And maybe disappointed. It was just a mess.

With his child stuck in the middle.

This was his worst nightmare. A family, kids—a wife, even—were not on his agenda.

"We used protection," he said numbly.

"Which isn't a hundred percent reliable. We were pretty careful, but…" Her hazel eyes met his. "Not careful enough, I guess. Believe me, this was not planned."

His suit jacket felt too tight, and his tie strangled his throat. But he kept his hands firm on the arms of the chair. His gaze stole to her midsection again, though most of it was hidden behind the desk.

His child. With a woman he barely knew, someone with whom he had simply enjoyed a few weeks during a summer trip. And he'd come here with the sole objective of hooking up with her again. He ran his hand over his face.

He should have known that someday his behavior was going to land him in trouble. That eventually his casual approach to relationships would come back to bite him. No words of *I love you*, no commitments, no strings. That was how he liked it. And even though he'd enjoyed his time here, a few states and an international border had made Tori Sharpe seem like a perfectly safe…distraction.

He wasn't really a player, but he'd classify his approach to romance as…cavalier. His best friend Cole called him a serial dater. Branson had silently agreed with the assessment. He hadn't had a relationship that had lasted over a month since college.

He let out a breath and tried to relax his shoulders. "Okay. So the news is out now, like it or not." He pinned her with his gaze. "And I have no idea what to do."

The lines in her face softened. "That's okay. I do. I don't expect anything from you, Jeremy. I'm not going to come after you for exorbitant amounts of child support or anything. I'm going to raise this baby right here. I have tons of friends I can count on, and my mom is here, and we'll be as happy as anything. I'll even sign papers if you want."

No child support? No contact? And raising the baby in this small town that was nearly dead in the off-season?

"Anything but that," he replied.

CHAPTER TWO

AFTER JEREMY'S LAST statement, tensions had ratcheted up again. Tori had asserted that nothing was going to be decided that afternoon and perhaps they could pick up the discussion later after they'd both had time to think. He hadn't looked happy, but Tori knew they could have gone around in circles indefinitely. It was going to take time to sort out, and she needed time to decide what she really wanted and how best to present it to Jeremy. Being caught on the fly had only made her panic, though she'd tried to cover it up as best she could.

She could compromise on a lot of things, but not on the basics. The baby would live here, with her. As far as his involvement went, that was negotiable. Now that he knew, she could hardly shut him out of everything and pretend he didn't exist if that wasn't what he wanted.

If she tried to cut him out of the baby's life, she had the suspicious feeling he'd start throwing his weight around. And he had the money and connections to make things difficult. The fantasy bubble in which she'd held the memories of their time together was truly popped. It was like her mom said—if it seemed too good to be true, it probably was.

What a tightrope she was going to have to walk. Hopefully he was in town for only a few days.

He'd gone to check in to his room and she logged in to the reservations system to get the details of his stay. To her dismay, she discovered he'd booked twelve days. That took them well into December. And it was more than enough time for things to go seriously wrong. She tapped her fingers on her desk. How the heck was she supposed to navigate this?

She thought back to earlier, when she'd admitted flat out that she'd lose in a power struggle. His gray eyes had looked so shocked that she'd even think such a thing. He'd run his fingers through his hair, and his throat had bobbed as he swallowed. Her words had left their mark, and it boded well as far as being able to reach him. He wasn't a cold and calculating monster, though she knew he was a tough negotiator when pushed. Watching him work closing deals last summer had shown her that, and she'd admired him for it at the time.

His wounded expression had also touched

something in her heart she wished didn't exist. She cared about him. Two weeks together in the summer had been more than enough time for her to develop feelings. Not love, certainly, but definitely affection. It hadn't all been sexual. He'd been charming, and funny, and smart. In fact, he'd been nearly perfect. Even if she'd been absolutely fine knowing their time together would be no more than a whirlwind fling, it was hard to erase all of those memories and see him dispassionately as the father of her unborn child. He wasn't just a sperm donor.

One morning they'd basked in the sunlight streaming through the bedroom window and he'd told her about why he loved real estate. It wasn't just about the bargaining or the money. As his fingers had traced down her arm, he'd said it was about finding homes for people, places where they belonged and could be happy. And when he'd realized he'd let her in, he'd immediately backtracked and said it was just a big bonus that his clients were all stinkin' rich.

But it had been a defense mechanism, she was sure. And she'd liked that glimpse into the man, and not just the fantasy.

Perhaps the best way to reach him was to approach the situation on a very human level. She could do that and still keep her other feelings locked away, right?

She put her hand on her tummy, wondering when she was going to start feeling the baby move. So far she had the bump but she hadn't really felt much. A few times she wondered if she might be feeling flutterings of movement, but she'd been told they were probably just gas.

Either way, she'd do what she had to in order to make sure her baby was loved and secure.

Whatever it took. Even being super nice to Jeremy Fisher.

The mile-long beach in front of the Sandpiper Resort was beautiful, even in late November. The waves were now more gray than blue, and the wind was raw, but there was a wildness to it that Jeremy loved, and the sound of the waves soothed his troubled mind.

Because he was, indeed, very troubled.

He'd left his running shoes on, meaning he'd have to shake them out later as the sand, even in the November chill, was still soft and thick. The wind whipped his hair around and made his jacket billow out behind him. Just a few months ago he'd walked this very beach with Tori. She'd worn a red bikini and had left her hair down, damp with seawater. They'd had so much fun; fun that had been missing in his life for too long. For those two weeks he'd put his troubles aside and let himself go. She had, too, or at least he'd thought so. They'd shared a blanket on the beach and soaked in the sun's rays; nibbled at a picnic prepared by the hotel kitchen; plucked seashells out of the damp sand that she said she was going to keep in her bathroom.

And then she'd taken him to her house and they'd spent hours exploring each other.

Just the memory made his body react, and he briefly considered jumping into the ocean, fully clothed, to cool off.

It had been easy being with her, because he'd known all along that he'd be leaving again. She wasn't his usual type of woman; his family and his money generally ensured that his dates were not of the small-town, girl-next-door variety, and being with her had been utterly refreshing. Now he'd be tied to her forever, because she was having his kid and there was no way on earth he would abandon his own child. He'd never planned to have any children, but he had to deal with the reality that he was going to be a father, and he was determined to be a better one than his own had been.

But how could he demand that Tori uproot her life? That wasn't fair either, and as much as Jeremy was used to getting what he wanted, he was a fair man. Or at least he wanted to think so.

He needed a plan. He was having a hard time

formulating one because he was still stuck on the idea that he was going to be a dad.

The idea was terrifying.

The raw wind bit through his jacket right to his bones as he carried on down the beach. His own parents had divorced when he was two, and he barely remembered his dad. Too often he'd been a pawn in battles between his parents, to the point where he'd often felt like a commodity rather than a son. His mother had remarried when he was four, and his siblings had been much older than him. By the time he'd started high school, his sister had been eighteen and starting college, and his brother, ten years his senior, had already been working in Silicon Valley. Jeremy had gone to prep school, away from home.

From the outside he'd certainly looked like a child of great privilege. There had always been money. There hadn't been a lot of love or warm fuzzies.

He stopped and stared out into the white-topped waves. Yesterday he'd watched as Tori cradled her gently swelling tummy and he'd seen the beatific expression on her face. That sort of maternal affection was completely foreign to him.

No matter what, he wouldn't take this baby away from her. And he or she would never be a pawn in some battle. Not if he could help it.

He started the mile-long walk back to the resort, his thoughts still churning. It would be different if Tori forced his hand. What if she tried to shut him out? He wouldn't try to shut her out, but he wasn't about to let her keep him from being a part of the baby's life. He didn't want his child growing up feeling unloved, or that he didn't care. The situation had to be handled with delicacy, that was for sure.

When he was almost to the resort, he looked up and saw a figure moving around the deck that in the summer had been a patio restaurant. The woman wore a heavy coat and a headband covered her ears, a dark ponytail keeping her hair tamed and out of her face in the brisk wind. The swirl of tension in his gut told him that it was Tori, even though her back was to him. On closer examination, he saw that she was stringing lights along the railing.

He jogged up to the main resort building and climbed the steps leading from the beach to the deck. "That's a cold job," he called out, and her head snapped up, the strands of lights forgotten in her fingers.

"Sorry," he apologized. "I didn't mean to startle you."

"I didn't hear you over the wind and waves."

He opened the gate and stepped onto the deck. He had gloves on his hands, but her fingers were bare and red. "You should be wearing gloves."

"They make my fingers too clunky," she answered, going back to the string of lights.

Jeremy moved forward and took them from her, then removed his gloves, tucked them beneath his arm, and took her hands in his. They were icy cold, and he chafed his fingers over hers to warm them. "Here. Put these on."

"Jeremy, I'm—"

"Shh. They're warm." He tugged the gloves over her fingers. They were too big, but she flexed her hands and he knew the material still held some of his heat.

Moments ago he'd been ready to take her on if she decided to play hardball. Now he was giving her gloves for her cold fingers. For a moment he wondered if he was a weak man, but then he reminded himself that being on good terms would only help matters in the end.

"Let me do a few of these. You show me how you want them."

"I'm just looping them on each post, see?" She held out a hand full of tie wraps. "Putting these on them, and snipping the ends with cutters."

Unease slipped through him. She was looping them, certainly, but he went back and saw how she did it and tried to re-create the same positioning of the string, though it took a few tries. And the tie wrap… He figured out that one end went through the other and he had to pull it tight, but it was a foreign sensation. He was not a handy kind of guy, in any sense. Someone had always done that sort of thing at home. He had many talents. Being handy was not one of them.

Ugh. He really was a spoiled brat, wasn't he?

She reached into her pocket for her cutters, then tightened his wrap a bit more and snipped the end. "Have you never hung Christmas lights?" she asked.

"First time," he admitted, pulling on the strand until it was taut again. His fingers were already getting cold; how had she managed to put this many up without getting frostbite? But he pushed on because he didn't want her to think he was a wimp or completely inept. Together they positioned, fastened and clipped the lights into place. Once they traded gloves so he could warm his hands, too, and then he put the lights up and over the arched entrance to the deck. "Will anyone even come out here?" he asked, trying hard not to shiver. He was pretty sure he couldn't feel his ears anymore.

"No. But we always put the lights up and a lit tree out here. It looks nice from the beach and also from the dining room."

He clapped his hands together for warmth. "You mean we still have to do a tree?"

"What's the matter, not used to the cold?"

New York got plenty cold in the winter, but the

icy wind off the ocean was going right through him today. When he didn't answer right away, she laughed—a soft, musical sound that suddenly made him feel lighter. "Your ears are pink. We'd better get you inside. Don't worry, we set up the tree inside and then move it out. Thanks for your help, though. My fingers appreciate it."

"You're welcome." Despite the cold, it had been kind of fun.

She looked at her watch. "It's nearly noon. Do you want to come in for some lunch? Or do you have appointments?"

He shrugged. "I don't have an appointment until two, so I have an hour to spare."

She opened the door that led from the deck to the dining room. "Our chef, Neil, does a curried carrot and ginger soup that is amazing. Definitely cold-weather comfort food."

They went inside and he watched as Tori went to the bar and spoke to the server behind the counter. When she came back, she led them to a table near the fireplace and hung her jacket over a chair. "Phew," she said, sitting down. "I'm not going to lie, that fire feels wonderful."

There were a handful of guests in the dining room, but it was otherwise quiet. "Not your busy time of year, huh?"

She shook her head as he took the chair opposite her. "No. The weekends are busier. People out for dinner, and our Sunday brunch is amazing." She looked up, and he got caught in her eyes again. Today her hazel eyes looked more green than brown, and her thick lashes made them seem bigger. He wondered if their baby would have her eyes.

"I'll have to try it while I'm here."

He sat back when the waitress came over with a basket of warm rolls and pats of butter. "Your lunch will be right out, Ms. Sharpe."

"Thank you, Ellen."

Tori looked up at him, a smile on her lips. "You warming up yet? Your ears aren't quite so pink."

He chuckled a little, his gaze stuck on her lips. Just his luck he couldn't quite forget kissing them. There could be none of that now. "The fire is helping. The wind is so bitter today."

"So why were you walking the beach?" she asked, picking up a roll and breaking it in half.

"Thinking," he replied, meeting her gaze. "I had a lot to think about."

"And did you come to any conclusions?"

Her voice was calm, but he could see a tightening around her mouth. She was nervous about this, too. It gave him a little comfort. The lives they'd both built—separately—were about to be disrupted.

"A few," he admitted. "But I'm not sure you're ready to hear them."

CHAPTER THREE

UNEASE SETTLED THROUGH HER, making her limbs feel heavy and her breath short. This was never going to be easy, but despite all the thinking she'd been doing the last twenty-four hours, she felt ill-prepared for whatever was going to come out of his mouth next.

She nibbled on a corner of the roll, though her appetite was diminishing rapidly. "Oh?" she asked, keeping her voice deceptively light.

He met her gaze and held it. "One thing is for sure, Tori—I can't go back to New York and pretend that this isn't happening. I'm going to be a father. I'm not going to abandon you or my child."

Tears stung her eyes and she looked down at the napkin in her lap. It was lovely to know that he accepted the pregnancy and wanted to be a part of their baby's life. But it stung that they were no more than an obligation to him; that he was tied to them out of duty and DNA and not affection.

"Thank you," she whispered.

"And whatever you need, you only have to ask. You need to know I'm willing and able to support you financially."

Financially. She clenched her fingers into fists under the table.

"Tori?"

She'd been silent so long he reached over and touched her arm, prompting her to look up. She took a deep breath, met his gaze and said quite clearly, "Thank you, Jeremy. But I'm quite able to provide for us."

His expression grew puzzled as his brows knit together. "Then what do you want from me?"

"Honestly? I don't know. Time, I suppose. To figure this out."

He looked at her tummy and then back to her face, and a hint of a smile quirked at the corner of his lips. "Well, we are on a bit of a ticking clock, don't you think? And it's halfway to midnight."

She raised her eyebrow in response. "I'm hardly Cinderella. Or a damsel in distress that needs rescuing."

At that moment their lunch was served; piping-hot bowls of soup along with bacon-and-avocado paninis that seemed to satisfy some sort of craving of Tori's right now.

"This smells delicious."

"It is. I'm kind of addicted to these sandwiches.

I'm not sure if it's the avocado or the bacon that the baby likes so much, but it's my favorite."

They ate in silence for a few moments, and then Jeremy spoke again. "This feels so weird. Last summer…"

His voice trailed away and Tori's cheeks heated. Last summer she'd felt about ten years younger and stupidly carefree. Days on the beach, toes in the sand, love in the middle of the day. She'd told herself she deserved a bit of fun, but she'd been careless. They both had.

"Last summer was just…what it was." She wiped her lips with her napkin and tried to calm the rapid beat of her heart. "We got carried away. We were impulsive, and now there are consequences. We can't be impulsive this time, Jeremy. We have to make the right decisions."

"I know."

She thought of her mom, who was both dismayed at how the pregnancy had occurred and ecstatic about being a grandmother. There were just the two of them now. She was an only child, a bit of a miracle baby, really, since her mother had been told she'd probably never conceive. Her grandparents lived in Newfoundland and she rarely saw them. Her father had died two years earlier. Tori felt a certain responsibility to be there for her mom. Without Tori, Shelley had no family.

She looked at Jeremy. "Do you have brothers and sisters?"

"One of each."

The topic had never come up during their few weeks of bliss. Now that Tori thought back to those sun-soaked days, she realized that anytime she had gotten close to talking about his family, he'd changed the subject. Even now, he didn't offer any explanations. Just "one of each."

"And your parents? Are they both back in New York?"

"My mother is in Connecticut. My father lives in the Virgin Islands. They divorced when I was little."

He picked up his sandwich and took a bite, but his face was set in a grim expression even as he chewed. Her heart sank a bit. It would be a shame if he wasn't close with his family. What would that mean for their child?

"Cousins? Favorite aunts and uncles?"

He swallowed and wiped his fingers on his napkin. "What's the point of this family tree examination?"

All the warmth from earlier was gone from his voice, and she withdrew a little bit. "We just… don't know much about each other, that's all. And it seems strange under the circumstances. Besides…" She lifted her chin a bit. "These people are going to be our baby's family, too. Isn't it right I know more about them?"

He took a drink of water and put down his glass, then placed his napkin on the table as he rose. "I'm sorry, but I really should head out to my appointment. Thank you for lunch."

He took a step to pass the table and she reached out to put a hand on his arm. "Is your family so bad you won't even talk about them?"

He looked down at her, and she couldn't read his eyes at all. They were flinty gray and shuttered, keeping her from seeing anything too personal. "It's not something to discuss over lunch."

"Then later?"

He moved his arm out from beneath her hand. "I've got to go, Tori."

The way he said her name at the end told her he wasn't as closed off as he appeared. Perhaps what they really needed was some time away from prying eyes to discuss properly what the pregnancy meant—to both of them.

"Drive carefully," she replied and shifted in her seat, letting him off the hook.

When he was gone she tried to finish her sandwich, but her appetite had gone with him.

The hot shower was exactly what Jeremy needed after the long day. This afternoon he'd visited three different properties along the South Shore, looking for the perfect home for his client, Branson Black, who was also a former classmate and one of his closest friends. Black was nearly as rich as Jeremy, but he wanted little to do with the money, which Jeremy couldn't quite understand. His instructions were to find a property with a view of the ocean and away from just about everything else. Jeremy was all about giving the client what he or she wanted, but he worried that Bran was trying to hide away from life and not just recover from recent trauma.

Still, he'd found one that he felt was perfect, and under three million. It even came with its own lighthouse, which, of course, was defunct but still lent the property an air of history and uniqueness. He had appointments to see several others during the week, though, before narrowing the choices down to send to Bran.

Being next to the ocean all day, walking the properties, had chilled him to the bone. He'd warmed himself during walk-throughs and by cranking the heat in the car, but the hot shower and warm hotel were more than welcome once he returned.

The hotel might be cozy, but Jeremy's thoughts were not.

He kept messing things up with Tori. He should have known that she'd start asking questions about his family. She was that type. Girl-next-door, nurturing, home-and-family type. He'd always been able to spot them because theirs had been so very different from his own upbringing. Last summer she'd talked about her mom a lot, and missing her dad, and Jeremy had always changed the subject. She didn't need to know that his dad had walked out when he was a little boy and that his mother hadn't been much of a mother at all; she'd left that to the nannies— plural, because his mother tended to hire young women looking to gain some "adventure" by working for rich families for a year or two and then moving on. Some had been nice. Some had been tolerable, more excited about the money and their days off. The last one had had an affair with his stepfather, and that had been the end of the nannies and the beginning of the talk about boarding school. His stepdad had stayed. Jeremy had been sent away.

But it had been a blessing, really. When he'd finished middle school, he'd been sent to out-of-the-way Merrick Hall. And there he'd found his family—of sorts. Including Branson.

He tugged on a warm sweater and called down to room service for dinner. When it was delivered forty minutes later, he opened the door to find Tori's soft face behind the cart.

"Room service," she said softly, and offered a timid smile.

He couldn't find it in himself to stay irritated. He opened the door wide and let her in, watching her hips sway as she moved the cart into the room. He swallowed thickly. Tori Sharpe was no less attractive now than she'd been five months ago. There was a subtle sexuality about her that was alluring. And when she turned around and the gentle swell of her tummy was visible, his heart gave a little thump. That was his child in there. He had no idea what to do but he knew for sure he wanted to be a better dad than his own had been.

"It's late. I didn't think you'd still be working," he said, then realized how critical he must sound right now. "Thank you for bringing it," he added, trying to be less of a jerk. After all, he'd walked out of their lunch like a coward.

"I waited for you to come back," she admitted, her dark eyes troubled. "I didn't like how we left things at lunch, and I wanted to say I was sorry for prying."

"You had a right to ask those questions. It's not your fault I don't like answering them."

She folded her hands in front of her. "You should eat while it's hot. Let me set this up for you."

He watched as she set a place at the small table and chair by the window of the suite, poured his beer into a glass and whisked the cover off his entrée to reveal a glistening steak surrounded by roasted potatoes, grilled asparagus and button mushrooms in garlic butter. It smelled heavenly, and his stomach growled in response.

"Have you eaten?"

"I have," she said. "So please, sit down. I'll leave you to it."

She turned to go and was almost to the door when he said, "Tori? Stay."

The moment she paused seemed filled with... well, surely not possibility? There was a change though, somehow. As if the invitation marked a willing step toward discussion. Intention, rather than dancing around the topic or taking the temperature of the situation.

And when she turned back around and faced him, his stomach quivered. He didn't let himself get too personally involved with anyone, but he was going to have to with her, wasn't he? At least if he wanted more of a relationship with his kid than sending a support check every month.

"Are you sure?"

He nodded. "I was rude this afternoon. I'm sorry about that."

She took a single step toward him. "Neither of us knows how to navigate this. It's an unusual situation."

He gestured to the seat across the table from

his food. "Come sit. Do you want some tea? Or anything else sent up?"

"There's water on the cart. I'll grab one of your glasses and have some. That's all I need."

He waited until she had her water and then they sat together. It felt wrong, eating while she wasn't, but the food was delicious and by her own admission she'd had dinner already. The asparagus was done to perfection and the steak mouthwateringly medium, just as he'd requested.

"Your chef is very good," he said. "This is delicious."

"Tastes here aren't terribly adventurous, so he does simple things well and adds a bit of flair when he can. But no one leaves hungry." She smiled. "Neil has been here a long time, and the rest of the kitchen staff have trained under him. It makes for a consistent culinary experience."

The resort wasn't as glamorous as some he'd stayed in, but he had no complaints.

"And you've been here a long time, too."

She lifted her water glass. "Since I was in high school. I started in housekeeping. Then moved to waitressing when I was legal age. Front desk for a while, too."

"You trained yourself to know the different departments," he observed, and her cheeks colored a little.

"I wanted to be in administration. For a while

I was the events manager, in charge of special functions. Then when the assistant manager retired, I applied for the job and got it. This week, I'm acting manager since Tom is away on vacation. Saint Lucia, lucky thing!"

"And your mom is here. You have strong ties."

"The strongest. My mom doesn't have anyone else, really. As far as family goes, that is. Of course, she has friends."

"As do you."

Her brow furrowed. "Well, yes."

"And so you probably wouldn't consider moving."

Her hand stilled halfway to the table, the glass trembling in her fingers. "Moving? As in…"

"Nearer to me. So our baby could be close to both parents."

"Not *with* you."

His eyes widened. Did she think he was going to ask her to move in with him? Or "do the right thing" and propose? Their affair had been amazing, but there wasn't love between them.

"This isn't the fifties. We don't have to get married to parent this child. But I did wonder if you'd consider moving somewhere closer to, well, me. Of course, I'd look after everything financially."

Her throat worked for several seconds while she studied her fingers, then looked up. Her eyes were clear and there was no censure on her face, either. "It's a generous offer, Jeremy. But my life is here, as you just heard. I'm truly glad you want to be a part of his or her life, but I'm not prepared to completely uproot mine to make that happen, any more than you're willing to uproot yours."

She was right. If the shoe were on the other foot, he'd never agree to leaving his life behind and moving to small-town Nova Scotia. They were from totally different worlds.

"I respect that," he said, putting down his knife and fork. "I really do. But I thought I should at least put the possibility on the table."

"Of course."

"We don't have to decide right away, right? You've got a few more months to go."

She nodded. Then her expression softened. "About today... I'm sorry if I picked at a sore spot. Was your childhood awful? Is that why you don't talk about your family?"

He sliced into the steak and considered. She was going to find out at some point, wasn't she? All she had to do was get on the internet and do a bit of digging and she'd find out who he was. "My older sister works on Wall Street. And my big brother moved to California straight out of MIT. He worked for a few start-ups right out of college and then started his own. Now he's CEO of a Fortune 500 tech company."

"Wow."

"Yeah. Being in property, I'm kind of the underachiever of the family."

"But property is a huge investment," she contradicted, and he was amused and a bit flattered that she jumped to his defense. "And you don't sell average houses. Your clientele are all rich, right?"

"Yeah. Dropping a few mil on a house is no big deal for them." He realized she had no idea exactly how wealthy he was, and it both amused and pleased him.

"It's a whole other world."

He looked at her and held her gaze. "They're people, just like anyone else. They have their own pressures, insecurities, heartache. It's true that money can't buy happiness, you know."

"But it sure can help take some of the stress off," she remarked, leaning back in her chair. "So how much are you worth, Jeremy?"

She said it lightly, teasing even, but he figured now was the time to be honest.

"One point two billion," he replied.

She burst out laughing, then stopped abruptly as he merely kept watching her. He knew it was a crazy sum of money. Some days he didn't believe it himself.

"Wait. You're not joking."

"No, I'm not."

"You've made that much money in realty?" Her lips dropped open in disbelief.

"Hardly." He pushed his plate away, leaving a few little potatoes, and reached for the beer. "But I had a big trust fund—the one thing my dad left me. And I have a sister on Wall Street who manages my money for me. Add all my assets together...and you get that number."

She breathed out a couple of curse words that made him grin. "I always knew you had money, but...holy—"

"Our child won't have to worry about a thing, and neither will you." On impulse, he leaned over and took her hand. "I don't know what this is going to look like, but I do know this. I promise that I will never abandon you or our kid. If that means we're just friendly and we co-parent, then that's how it'll be. But if you need anything at all, you just have to pick up the phone. I'll be there for you."

He meant every word. He also knew that what he'd just said had essentially tied him to her for the rest of his life.

What had he just done?

CHAPTER FOUR

TORI TRIED TO quell the thrill that slid through her as Jeremy took her hand and promised to be there for her and their child. He was a tough man to resist at any time, but right now, with her hand in his, and the knowledge that he was a freaking billionaire swimming through her brain, she was quite overwhelmed.

She didn't care that he had bags of money. It wasn't that. It was just that she'd never met anyone quite this rich before. She certainly hadn't known last summer. It shouldn't change him in her eyes, but it did. He was so out of her league.

Not as a person; she knew that money and character were two very different things. But in worldly ways, he was on a whole other plane of existence.

"I don't know what to say," she responded, biting down on her lip. "I had no idea that… Well, Jeremy." She let out a big breath. "I'll make you a promise in return. I promise that I will never exploit the fact that you have money. I don't want us to use money against each other, you know? Either how much we have or the lack of it."

"Me, either. I want us to figure this out in a way that's best for our baby."

"You really do believe everything, don't you? About it being yours and everything?"

He let out a sigh. "I didn't react so well when I saw you were pregnant. But yes, I believe you."

"When the baby is born we can do a DNA test. I wasn't going to do an amnio if I could avoid it. The idea freaks me out."

"A what?"

"An amniocentesis. It's a test where they insert this needle and withdraw a bit of the amniotic fluid—"

He shuddered. "Ouch, and gross."

She laughed. "Yeah. And there are some risks involved. I didn't want to take any chances."

"So you really do want the baby."

She nodded. "I do. It wasn't planned, but I… I don't have much family. And I like children, a lot."

Her clock hadn't really begun ticking yet, not at twenty-eight, but she couldn't lie. She'd been starting to think about a family the last few years. This pregnancy was inconvenient and a shock, yes. But also a blessing.

"I'm not close to mine, as you might have gathered." He took a long pull of his beer and pursed his lips. "I'm closest to my sister, and we both live in New York so we see each other most of anyone. But my brother... He's on his third marriage already and does his own thing."

"And your mom?"

"She's still at the family home in Connecticut. Married to my stepfather. Socializing with the right people, that sort of thing. My dad left and she got the house. Not much else, but we all had our trust funds and she married again within a few years. She made sure she was looked after."

There was a bitterness in his voice he couldn't disguise, and Tori wondered about the little boy he must have been. "I take it she wasn't the nurturing type?"

He laughed—a short, mocking sound. "Not an ounce," he replied, then drained his beer glass. He got up, went to the minibar, and took out a bottle of Cape Breton whiskey, adding a significant splash to a highball glass. He swirled it for a moment before turning and looking at her. "My mom was a social climber. I didn't know it then, but I know it now. I see the type. And when Dad left, she lost her ticket. She would have had to sell the house and finish bringing us up on her own. Instead she married Bruce, and since she came with the house, he brought the rest of his money and status was restored. Some investments on her part paid for our college. Bruce, apparently, was more than happy to pay my four years of tuition to boarding school. I wasn't really home after I finished eighth grade."

He downed the whiskey in one gulp, and poured another.

She sat quietly. First of all, clearly the topic was painful to him, because he was fortifying himself with alcohol. And secondly, as much as his words were delivered in a factual, who-gives-a-care way, she could tell that the lack of affection had left its mark on him.

Tori couldn't imagine not loving your own child, or considering them in the way. Or sending them away, at such a difficult age.

"Where did you go?"

"Merrick Hall, an all-boys school in Connecticut. Very *Dead Poets Society* with old buildings and rituals and dormitories. Top-notch learning, though." He must have seen her alarmed look because he attempted a smile and went to her. "It was fine, really," he assured her. "I belonged there. I met my best friends there. And despite my cold family, I do have some really great friends."

Tori let out a breath. "Oh, of course you do. But now I understand your reluctance. Do you still see your mother? Your stepfather?"

He nodded. "Now and again. Despite everything, she *is* my mother."

Tori was glad. Estrangement could be such a horrible thing.

"So now you know what I didn't want to talk about over lunch." He sipped at his drink this time, to her relief. "I don't know what kind of father I'll make. But I promise to try. Any kid of mine is going to feel wanted and loved. Not in the way."

He said it with such finality that Tori's heart broke just a little. She'd been brought up in a home with so much love. It was incomprehensible to think of a parent being so careless and dismissive, but she knew it happened.

She looked up at Jeremy, at his dark hair and stormy eyes and cheeks, slightly flushed from the day's wind and the warm whiskey. She wanted to reach up and brush the errant curl off his forehead, to smooth the creases on his forehead, to see his lips curve in a smile again. But she kept her hands to herself, knowing that touching him, kissing him, would only make matters more complicated than they already were.

"Then we're going to be fine," she whispered, twisting her fingers together to keep from reaching out. "Because that's what I want, too. And we'll figure out the rest of the details somehow."

Their gazes held for a few seconds, and then a few seconds more, long enough for something to stir between them. Her body remembered what his felt like and ached to feel it pressed against her again. She remembered how he tasted, the way he angled his head to kiss her, and how he nibbled at her lower lip before taking a kiss deeper.

She stepped back, unwilling to cross that line again. "I should go. It's getting late and I'm on shift again tomorrow."

"When do you get a day off?"

"On Thursday, when Tom is back from his holiday."

"I'll have narrowed down some properties by then. Why don't you come along for some second walk-throughs? Some of these places are really stunning. You can tell me where we should eat lunch and we can make a day of it."

She frowned. "Are you sure that's a good idea?"

"How are we going to manage to parent together if we can't get through a day in each other's company?"

He made sense, even though Tori knew it was simplifying the matter. "Well, all right. If the weather is good. And as long as nothing comes up here."

"Of course."

She began to clear his plate and dinner mess and put it back on the room service cart. "You don't have to do that," he said.

She laughed. "Sure I do. I work here, remember? I'll drop it off at the kitchen and then go home."

He opened the door for her and she wheeled the cart out into the hall. Then she looked back at him. "Thanks for telling me about your family, Jeremy," she said. "I know you didn't want to."

"It's out there now," he replied, leaning on the door. "Just please…don't judge me on the basis of my relatives. I've tried very hard to be…different."

"I judge a person on what I see them do," she answered, and gave him a smile. "So far you're in the clear."

He smiled back then, a sexy sideways little slice of amusement. "I'll see you soon." Then with a little laugh, he backed up and shut the door.

She wheeled the cart down the hallway to the elevator while trying to calm her thrumming pulse. Amity was better than enmity, for sure, but how was she going to deal with a smiling Jeremy? Because she still found him incredibly attractive. Still got that light feeling in her chest when he smiled at her. And with their baby on the way, she couldn't afford to let her head get into the clouds.

Life wasn't made of fairy tales. It just had reality, and this was hers. She'd better figure it out.

* * *

Thursday dawned bright and clear, and after a brief meeting with Tom to bring him up to speed, Tori bundled up in her warm parka and gloves. Her knee-high boots and leggings were comfortable and warmer than she would have been in a skirt. The jacket was a bit snug around the waist, and she tugged on the zipper to get it over her growing bump. She supposed a new coat would be on the shopping list, but she hated spending the money on something she'd wear for only one winter.

Jeremy was waiting in the lounge sipping on coffee when she emerged from her office. To be honest, she was looking forward to the morning. There were worse things than wandering through luxury homes. She loved flipping through magazines and seeing the fancy decor. Now she could see some in person. Maybe even get some ideas for the hotel.

"Hi there."

Jeremy turned around and she tried not to stare. He was in suit pants and shoes, with a soft wool coat and plaid scarf around his neck. His hair was finger-combed back from his face, making it seem groomed but carelessly so.

"Hi, yourself. Do you want a tea for the road? Something hot?"

"No, I'm fine. I had a decaf in the office with Tom this morning. You're ready?"

"Just let me get this in a travel cup and I will be." He flashed her a smile—another jolt to her heart—and beckoned for the waitress to grab him a cup. Within seconds he had his hand at the base of Tori's spine, solicitously leading her out to his rental.

It was a freaking Jaguar.

He held the door and she slid into the sleek interior, the soft leather cradling her like it was shaped to her bottom. It was cold, but in moments he had the heater turned up and her heated seat on. A map on the console flashed and he hit a preset for one of the properties, and then they were on the road, heading toward Bridgewater.

"Where are we going first?"

He tapped the wheel along with the satellite radio station that was playing. "A house in the Pleasantville area. On the LaHave River."

"I know the area."

"Branson's looking for a place to…well, regroup, I guess. He's had a rough year."

"Branson?"

"My client. And my friend."

"How has his year been rough?"

Jeremy frowned. "It's not really my place to say, you know? He's a private guy, and I respect that. But if he wants to be invisible, I'm going to help him get what he needs and make sure it's a good investment. I don't think he'll live here full-time, at least not after a while." He looked over at Tori. "As his friend, my hope is he'll put himself back together, and use this place as a summer home. Get back to throwing parties and having fun. He needs to smile again."

Tori wondered what could be so awful that Jeremy couldn't talk about it, but she respected his desire to protect his friend's privacy. "He's one of your Merrick friends?"

Jeremy nodded. "Yep."

The drive to Pleasantville wasn't long, and Jeremy had just finished his coffee when they pulled through iron gates into a long drive.

At the top was a gorgeous gray-shingled house with a three-car garage attached. Tori's breath caught—it was so cozy looking despite its size. "How much did you say this was?" she asked, scanning the yard, which was covered with a thin layer of snow.

"One point four."

"It doesn't seem quite that grand."

He chuckled. "You wait. It's three acres on the water, and the bottom floor is a walkout. It looks much bigger from the back than the front."

He led her to the front door and then opened the lockbox, giving them entry. She stepped inside and gasped. It was so airy and light and beautiful!

She took off her boots and left them on the rug at the door, then stepped onto the silky hardwood. "Okay, so you're right. It's bigger inside than it looks from the outside."

He took her on a walk-through. The kitchen walls were a pale yellow, with white cupboards and woodwork, and granite countertop along the counters and the center island. Stainless steel appliances gleamed in the morning sun, and Tori couldn't stop herself from oohing over the double wall ovens. Their footsteps echoed through the rest of the downstairs rooms, and then they went up the curved staircase to the next level, where several of the rooms had windows overlooking the water. Even the en suite bathroom was perfectly situated so that one could soak in the oversize tub and look out at the river and a huge tree standing sentinel by a small dock.

"A dock for a boat."

"Yes. And a short sail down the river to the ocean. What do you think?"

She laughed. "It's beautiful and ginormous. You've seen my cottage. What would I ever do with this much room?"

She could feel his gaze on her as she wandered to the windows of the master bedroom again.

"But it is lovely. Truly. And despite the size, it feels like a home. That's nice."

They put their shoes back on and wandered around the outside for a bit, and Tori discovered he was right. The house's most impressive aspect was from the river, looking in. Three stories of large windows shone in the sunlight.

"Kids could play here," she mused. "It's just a gentle slope to the water. And gardens. Are there gardens in the summer?"

"Yes, though, of course, we can't see them now."

"Wow. Is this the kind of place you always show, Jeremy?"

He laughed. "Yes and no. This type of property would cost a lot more in other areas. And some of the properties in Manhattan would stop your heart."

"Like yours?"

He shrugged. "I live on the Upper East Side. It's not known for being cheap."

She put her hands in her pockets and squinted up at him. "How much was your place?"

He met her gaze. "Just over four."

"Million?"

He nodded. "It's pretty modest. I didn't need someplace huge and empty, you know?"

"Oh, my—"

He burst out laughing then and she joined in,

just because it all seemed so incredulous and the sound of his laughter filled her with some sort of strange joy.

"Come on," he said, holding out his hand. "Let's go see the next one."

They left the house behind and journeyed a short way to a property that was more isolated and right on the ocean. A small cliff separated the property from the sea, and at once Tori was taken with it.

"If the last one was homey, this one is wild," she said, stepping out of the car. The wind off the water whipped her hair off her face and she turned into it, loving the feel even though it wrapped around her with icy-cold fingers. "It's incredible here!"

She had to shout to be heard, but she could see the look of admiration on Jeremy's face and knew this was a favorite of his, too. She rounded the hood of the car and met him on the crushed walkway to the house. "You love it, don't you?" she asked, tucking a swath of hair behind her ear.

"I do. And you'll see why in a minute."

When they got inside, he swept out an arm. "Now do you see?"

Past the foyer was a center area with a small table in the middle, holding a bouquet of flowers. And to the left was the beginning of a circular staircase that climbed up...and up...and up. Tori went to the middle and looked up. There was a skylight at the top, so that a perfect column of light fell from the roof right to the spot where the table sat, and the column was framed by the dark wood of the railings and the creamy white of the steps' risers.

"That," she said definitively, "is a conversation piece. Amazing."

"Isn't it? And there's a sauna downstairs, and an exercise room…"

"No private beach?"

"There is, but it's not direct access because of the cliffs. I'd show you, but I'm afraid it's a bit icy and I don't want you to fall."

There was a room on the side that was rounded, like a hexagon, windows all around to provide a 270-degree view. A stone fireplace was in one "corner," with granite along the bottom of the wall, giving it a rustic feel.

"Can you imagine," she said, unable to keep the awe out of her voice, "sitting here with the fire blazing and a storm outside, with a glass of wine and a book?"

"Yeah," he said softly. "I can."

Their eyes met. This house was not for them. They weren't even a *thing*. But walking through it together was…intimate in a way she hadn't expected. She cleared her throat. "Come on, show me the rest, then."

On top of the porch was a railed deck, with French doors leading from the master bedroom. Tori had never seen such luxury in her life. Even with the furniture moved out, the rooms were commanding in their size and the views were incomparable. Two more huge bedrooms, each with their own bath, finished the upstairs.

"You want to recommend this one, don't you?" she asked. "You like it a lot."

He nodded. "I think it suits Branson, but it's pretty isolated. And did I mention the best part? It has its own lighthouse at the edge of the property. Look."

He pointed southeast, where the land jutted out into the ocean. It wasn't huge, but sure enough, a red-and-white lighthouse stood sentinel, looking a little worse for wear. "Is it still active?"

"No," he replied, sounding disappointed. "But the owner assures me it's still in working order. Solid as the cliff it's built on."

It was undeniably romantic. Who wouldn't want to have their own lighthouse?

"Can we see it?"

He shook his head. "It's a different key, and I don't have access to it."

"Oh."

They wandered through some more, and Tori was quite taken with it all. When he told her the price tag, she laughed and said a girl could dream, but then laughed again and asked what she'd ever do with all that space. It needed people to fill it up. It needed not only priceless views but life and laughter.

They headed back toward Liverpool, went past the exit and on to a third house that was on Jeremy's short list. She didn't like it nearly as well, though. It was in the same price range as the others, but was a little too avant-garde for her in its design. The house itself looked like a giant block dropped on the sand, and inside it was nearly as austere.

"You don't like it," he said as they walked through.

"It has every amenity a person could want," she remarked, "but I feel off balance. I don't feel at home here. And I know it sounds weird, but I feel like it could just tip over into the Atlantic."

He laughed. "Fair enough."

She put her hands on the cold railing of the stairs and said, "It's the kind of place that people call 'innovative' and 'remarkable' but there's not a lot of comfort here."

"So let's take it off the list."

She looked at him with some alarm. "Oh, gosh, don't take anything I say into account! I have no idea about real estate."

He came over and stood next to her, his hand on the railing close to hers. "But you do know what goes into making people feel comfortable and at home. It's part of why the Sandpiper is such a success. That's what my friend needs right now."

Her heart stuttered a bit. He was a surprise for sure. "Which one gets you the biggest commission?"

He laughed. "This one, actually. But it's never about that."

"It's not?"

"I don't need the money. But I like finding people places to live. I like to imagine them happy there."

"You surprise me, Jeremy."

"Why?"

She put her hand on his chest. "Because in there is the heart of a man who is looking for a home."

His face closed off immediately and he stood back. "That's just you being sentimental."

She'd touched a nerve; it didn't take a genius to figure that out. She dropped her hand. "Oh, maybe. I still think it's nice that you think about what suits the person and not just the biggest payoff."

He lifted his chin, gesturing toward the front door. "Should we find some lunch?"

Her stomach had been growling for an hour, so she readily agreed. "I know just the place."

He followed her outside, and she waited while he locked up. All the while Tori realized she was getting a better glimpse of what made Jeremy Fisher tick. And so far, what she saw made her heart soften. He could deny it all he wanted, but she'd been right. He was looking for home.

She'd always known what home meant. She'd always been wanted and nurtured and valued. What must it be like to have to search for those things?

CHAPTER FIVE

JEREMY WAS STILL shaken by Tori's observation back at the house. Was she right? Did everything come down to wanting to find a place he could call home? He'd done that, hadn't he? He loved his place, with the view of Central Park and the bustle of New York all around him. He was in the middle of it all. Work, restaurants, theater, museums.

But still, there was something missing. And how astute of Tori to realize it.

He buckled his seat belt and turned to her. "Okay, so where are we going?"

She took him to a little hole-in-the-wall restaurant with scarred wood tables and plastic tablecloths, and ordered them both fish and chips. "It's the house specialty," she insisted, and when the food came he goggled at the size of the platter. The whole plate was covered in crispy fries, with two pieces of battered fish on top, a paper cup of tartar sauce and a dish of coleslaw on the side.

"Vinegar?" the waitress asked, as she put down the steaming plates.

"Oh, yes, please."

Jeremy watched as Tori liberally shook vinegar on her fish and fries. "Come on," she said, grabbing her paper napkin and putting it on her knees. "Dig in."

He cut a piece of fish off with his fork and popped it in his mouth. Delicious. Light batter, perfectly crispy and flaky haddock inside. "Mmm."

"See?" She grinned at him as she speared a fry and dipped it in some ketchup.

He took another bite, then ate a fry and then tried some of the tangy coleslaw. Everything was amazing. He was glad he'd had only a fruit cup at breakfast with his coffee. The portions were huge.

"Why didn't we come here last summer?" he asked. It was close to her place, close to the Sandpiper.

"Because you can't get in the door here in the summertime. It's packed." She grinned up at him and let out a breath. "I need to slow down."

"Don't do it on my account." Truthfully, her love of food amused him. The last few dates he'd been on, the women had barely tasted their food and then insisted they were full. It had never made sense to him. People needed to eat to survive. It was also an experience to be enjoyed. Seeing Tori's grin as she bit down on a french fry made him happy for some reason.

"You're probably used to nicer restaurants," she said, pausing to take a drink of water. "Honestly, last summer I had no idea you were so rich. I would have recommended a few places. Particularly in Halifax."

He met her gaze. "At the time I was happy with whatever filled my hunger."

Her cheeks colored as she interpreted a double meaning he hadn't intended. But it was true. He'd been hungry for her. He still was, if he were being honest with himself. Knowing she was carrying his child only made her more beautiful, if that were possible. He had no trouble remembering the taste of her lips or the softness of her skin, the scent of sunscreen filling the air and the tangle of her hair in his hands. It was what had driven him to come back here in the first place. Branson's request had simply given him the excuse.

He shifted in his chair and dug into the fillet once more. Then he changed the conversation to safer topics, like the houses they'd already looked at. "You're going to recommend the one on the bluff, aren't you?" she asked.

"I think so, yes. I'll show him all three and give him my impressions, but overall I think that's what he'll pick."

"It was my favorite. I love how the ocean is so wild there, right on the point."

They'd made it through their fish and half the fries when Tori pushed her plate back. "Okay, I really have to stop if I'm going to have dessert."

He gawped. "Dessert?"

She laughed. "Yes. Because they make all their pies on-site and the coconut cream is my favorite."

He wasn't sure where he was going to put it, and he wouldn't have to eat for the rest of the day, but when the waitress came back, they ordered pie—the coconut cream for her and butterscotch for him, something he'd never had before. He had another coffee and she ordered a decaf, and they lingered a long time, sipping and picking at their dessert.

"This was nice," she said, absently fluffing her fork through some of the cream on top of her pie. "I think it bodes well for us getting along."

"Me, too. Though we didn't really talk about the future."

Her face turned troubled, with her lips tightening and her lashes cast down. He wondered why she did that, because he'd noticed it a few times now when there was the potential for conflict.

"Hey," he said softly, making her look up at him. "We'll get there. I've got more time here. Another week, anyway. I've got to go up to Halifax for a few days, too. You can take some time, and I will, too, to see if we can come up with a plan."

She nodded. "I know. It's fine, really. I just realized that this really wasn't how I'd planned to start a family. With his or her parents living in different countries."

"It's not ideal, but it's the reality we have to work with." At her downcast expression, he put his hand over hers. "Hey. Look on the bright side. I have the means to come visit, or have you come to New York. That sounds okay, right? We won't have to stress over money."

Her eyes brightened. "You mean you'd be okay with us staying here?"

He hadn't meant to agree to that so readily. Truthfully, he'd thought about how great it would be to have her move to New York so he could see his kid whenever he wanted. But he didn't want to get into that now, and mar the great day they'd been having. "There are a lot of options," he deflected, pulling his hand away and reaching for the last of his coffee. "So maybe what we need to do is think about what we each want and then sit down and have a discussion about it. See if we can find some middle ground."

"That sounds fair," she agreed. "I mean, so far we've managed not to argue about anything, and that's quite an achievement, considering."

He nodded, but something felt a little bit off. Like they hadn't argued…yet. And that something was going to come along and cause some friction, and he really didn't want that to happen. He didn't want to argue with her at all. Quite the contrary.

Jeremy frowned as he picked up the check. That was part of the problem, wasn't it? He still desired her, and now that they were spending more time together, he was discovering he still liked her, too. The woman he'd met last summer was the real Tori—smiling and easygoing, easy to be with, and a knack for making him smile. He'd been drawn to her charm and easy laugh, and had felt like he could simply be himself.

The combination made her more dangerous than she could imagine. Because the last thing he wanted was a ready-made family. He didn't know the first thing about how real families worked. His had always been dysfunctional. His most normal relationship had been with the gardener who had come around twice a week to look after the grounds and cut the grass.

Lord, what would Mr. Adley have to say about this predicament?

He'd tell him to do the right thing. The only trouble was, Jeremy had no idea what the right thing might be. It certainly wasn't a slapped-together marriage for the sake of a baby. For a marriage, there needed to be love, and Jeremy was relatively certain that he wasn't capable of that particular emotion.

They got in the car and headed back toward the hotel, where Tori would be able to pick up her car and head home. When they were maybe five minutes away, Tori sat up straight in her seat and pointed. "Slow down…there." She looked over at him and then pointed again, right at a small for-sale sign on a stake at the roadside. "Turn in here, Jeremy. Please!"

She said it with such urgency that he immediately braked and turned into the side road. "What are you looking for?"

"There was a for-sale sign, and there are only a few houses in here. I'm curious."

They'd finished their viewings, and it was still early, so he figured he might as well indulge her. "It's definitely off the beaten path."

"And straight down to the beach. Not the one by the inn, but a kilometer or so down the coast. It's not as big, but it's lovely. And it's on private property."

They found the for-sale sign close to the end of the lane, but the gate was closed. Tori looked so disappointed that he picked up his cell and dialed the number for the agent.

Then he turned to Tori with a smile. "He can

be here in twenty minutes. It's vacant—do you want to get out and walk the property?"

"I could stand to walk off some lunch," she replied, her eyes brightening again. "I'm gonna confess, Jeremy. I've always wanted to see this property. I've seen it from the water. I had no idea it was for sale, though."

"Then let's go."

He parked the car along the side of the lane, then took Tori's arm as they navigated their way around the small gate that was more for show than security. The drive was about a hundred and fifty yards long through a stand of trees, but then it opened up to a cleared yard and a property that was smaller and less grand than the others they'd seen, but impressive just the same.

"Oh, wow," Tori breathed, letting go of his arm as she moved forward. "Look at that."

The outside of the house was done in gray siding with white trim, with an oversize front door and stone steps and a stone walkway leading toward the drive. He'd seen and dismissed this property listing earlier in the week; at under three thousand square feet and a price tag below a million, it was less than what Branson was looking for. That didn't detract in any way from its charm. Under the film of snow, they saw stone gardens dotted with evergreen shrubs, and other areas that would no doubt sprout into a profusion of perennials come spring. The back of the house faced the water, and a path that ended in a set of steps led to the white-sand beach below. A quick assessment told Jeremy that the property probably included about three hundred feet or more of shoreline.

Tucked away in a corner was another smaller building, what Jeremy would have assumed was a converted boathouse. It too was gray, but with shaker shingles and a charming red front door. He was acutely aware of Tori at his side, eyes wide, falling in love with the place.

Her current house was about the size of the boathouse, certainly under a thousand square feet. Charm galore, but tiny.

"Oh, isn't this lovely?" She peeked into the front window. "It could be a guesthouse, or…" She turned to him, her eyes bright. "Something the owners could rent out or something. I mean, it's nicer than renting a room or basement. Guests would have their own space. I wonder if there's a little kitchen. It's cute as anything."

She was beautiful like this, so animated and with her eyes full of possibilities. It was what made her sweet, what made her entirely suited for her job at the Sandpiper. As she circled the little house, he realized with a sinking heart that she belonged here. She wasn't the kind to be happy in the city, was she? She loved the ocean, the open spaces, the wildness. It was as different from New York as sun from rain.

And he couldn't live here. Oh, financially he didn't need to work another day in his life if he didn't want to. But he'd be miserable otherwise. He needed a purpose. A challenge.

By the time she'd finished examining the lot, the Realtor arrived and was ready to show them the house. Inside was just as stunning as he'd imagined, with surprises in some of the detail, such as the iron-and-glass doors to a hidden patio. The iron was in the pattern of lilies, scrolling up through the glass. It was one of the nicest custom-made pieces he'd seen, and that was saying something. There were three large bedrooms upstairs, sweeping views, a chef's delight of a kitchen, and a garden with a stone firepit in the back.

"Oh, look. That's so pretty! And you could put chairs around it and have fires and roast marshmallows in the summer. And hear the ocean." Tori stood at the window, her face nearly touching the glass. "I know you said it wasn't on your list, but this is my favorite one yet."

"It's a bit small for the client. But you're right. It's a wonderful property. How long has it been on the market?"

The Realtor, who'd been wisely letting the house speak for itself, stepped forward. "Since September."

"Really." Jeremy lifted an eyebrow.

"It's not really a seller's market at the moment, as I'm sure you know." There was no harm in saying it, Jeremy knew exactly what the market was like and the other man knew it. "But the owners don't want to sell it for less than it's worth."

Of course not. And in truth, they could have added a good fifty-to-one-hundred thousand to the price and it would still be a good deal.

"I'll keep it in mind for other clients," Jeremy said, offering his hand. "Thanks for coming out today."

"My pleasure."

They stepped outside the house again and walked down the lane to where they'd parked the car. Tori lifted her hand in a friendly wave as the Realtor passed them on the way by. He smiled to himself; it was such a small-town thing to do.

They settled back into his car and started on the short drive back to the hotel. Tori sank into the seat and let out a sigh, resting her hand on her tummy. It was such a maternal gesture that his heart wrenched a little. She was going to be a good mother. There was genuine warmth and gentleness to her and he was at least thankful that his child would be in a happy, nurturing environment.

He cast his eyes back onto the road again. He

was already thinking in terms of his child living with her as if everything was already settled. Was that really what he wanted? To just back off and leave his kid here, while he returned to his previously scheduled life, with occasional visits so his son or daughter at least knew what he looked like?

He thought back to his upbringing, and his gut twisted. He actually couldn't remember what his father looked like, and it had taken many, many years for him to stop hoping that one day Brett Fisher would show up for his birthday or for Christmas, and take him away from the cold, lonely life he led. He refused to let any kid of his feel that way—always looking out the window, wondering if his father would come, disappointed when he didn't, only to have his hopes raised and dashed again and again.

What was the alternative?

They arrived back at the hotel and he got out and opened Tori's door before she had a chance to. She smiled up at him and his stomach twisted again, this time not out of pain but out of confusion. In some ways Tori was a stranger. They'd spent a few weeks having some fun, and now a few days talking. But in other ways, she was more than that. His feelings were complicated by desire and concern and, he realized, a bit of fear.

Because he liked her, dammit. And wanted

her. And the baby they'd made would join them together forever.

"What's wrong?" she asked, putting her hand on his arm, concern etching her face. "You're frowning."

"Just thinking," he replied, but consciously relaxed his features. "I should probably go up and put my thoughts together for Branson, and give him a call."

"Right. I keep forgetting today was work for you." She smiled, then looped her arm through his as they walked toward the lobby doors. "It was fun for me."

He tried to ignore how good her arm felt around his, her body pressed close to his side. "It was for me, too. Not every day is like this, though."

"Do you think your friend will put in an offer?"

"Perhaps."

"Why Nova Scotia, instead of somewhere else? I mean, there's Cape Cod. Or the Maine coast. What about the Hamptons? Don't all the richest people live in the Hamptons?"

She was so sweet and artless. She was looking up at him with a playful smile and he fought the urge to simply turn her into his arms and kiss her lips. "I think there's a family connection somehow," he replied, swallowing against the urge to make a move. And that was all he'd say about

Branson's connection to Nova Scotia. The rest would require explaining about events of recent months, and he valued Bran's privacy too much.

They stepped into the lobby, straight into warmth and hospitality and holiday cheer. A new addition—a ten-foot Christmas tree—was front and center, with sparkling white lights and blue plaid ribbon wrapped around its evergreen fullness. Clear, silver and blue ornaments shone from the tiny lights. "The Nova Scotia tartan," he murmured, nodding at the tree. "The ribbon. Whose idea?"

"Every year a different department gets to decorate the tree. This year it was housekeeping." She let go of his arm and walked to the tree, then plucked off an ornament and shook her head. "Oh, look at these," she said, holding it out in her hand.

He took it from her palm and turned it over in his fingers. The ball was white but transparent, and in silver paint was the word *Dream*.

There were others, they discovered. Some said *Rest*. Others *Relax* and *Indulge*. "I bet Miriam made these," Tori murmured, hanging one back on the tree. "She's amazing."

His mother would die before having handmade ornaments on her tree, and yet here he was in a luxury hotel and it was celebrated, not discouraged. The ornaments were as nice as any he'd seen, simple but elegant. At the top of each one was a perfect bow made from the same tartan pattern.

"You have some talented staff." He ran his fingertips over the sharp needles of the tree. "And you let them thrive."

"Everyone brings talents to the table. What kind of place would we be if we didn't take their ideas into account? Some of them are very, very good."

"You're incredible," he murmured, standing way too close to her. As if they suddenly realized it, he took a step back and Tori shifted away. But then the distance gave him a chance to see what was above her head. A large sprig of fresh mistletoe hung from the archway, and Tori was directly beneath it.

Before he could talk himself out of it, he stepped up to her and put his hand on the nape of her neck.

Alarmed eyes met with his. "What are you doing?" she whispered.

And then he pointed up, to the mistletoe above their heads. And when she looked back at him again, the confusion was gone and her face reflected back to him what he was feeling. Longing and fear together.

He leaned forward and touched his lips to hers, softly, testing. She was stiff, as if holding her breath, but the moment he paused and slid his fingers an inch through her hair, she relaxed and her lips opened a little. Just a bit, but enough that their mouths fitted together with a sweetness that shook him to the soles of his feet.

This woman. This moment. Carrying his child.

His head said he should not be kissing her. But to his heart it felt…right.

He didn't let the kiss linger too long; he slid his fingers over the curve of her neck and moved away, a few inches at a time, marveling at the quick beat of his heart from such an innocent bit of contact. Her cheeks were flushed and her lips pink and plump, open as if in surprise.

"I couldn't let perfectly good mistletoe go to waste," he murmured, and he ran his tongue over his bottom lip. It was a mistake, because the taste of her lingered there. He'd be a liar if he said he didn't want more.

"Then I think we should just say Merry Christmas and good-night," she replied, taking a shaky breath.

"It's not even dinnertime yet."

"Then…goodbye, then. I mean… Damn. I said *then* twice. I just mean…"

Her stammer was adorable, and told him she was just as affected as he was.

"I'll see you later. *Then.*" He added the last word and smiled, and before he could change his mind, walked to the stairs that would take him to his suite.

What she did for the rest of the evening was none of his business. None at all.

CHAPTER SIX

SATURDAY AFTERNOON TEA had become a weekly ritual, as long as Tori's mom wasn't on shift at the hospital. This weekend was no different from any other, except that Tori was anxious about telling her mom that Jeremy was in town. While Shelley was supportive, she wasn't a fan of how the pregnancy had happened, during a summer fling. Neither was Tori, to be honest. It would be different if it was an accident in an actual relationship based on love and not just… lust. But they had both agreed that since nothing could be changed, it was about looking to the future.

Now she was sitting in her mom's living room, nibbling on a gingersnap as her mom brought in a teapot and a little jug of milk, no sugar. Neither of them liked it in their tea.

Tori poured a cup and handed it to her mom, then poured one for herself. She took a sip of the hot brew and felt her muscles relax. There was nothing like a cup of tea to settle her thoughts.

"You're feeling okay?" Shelley said, looking over the rim of her mug with worried eyes. "You look a little pale. Is your iron low?"

"A little tired, maybe. I've had a lot on my mind lately. But everything's fine. I go for my ultrasound in a few days."

"When?"

"Tuesday."

"I'm on day shift. I can see if someone will switch if you want company."

Her mom's eyes lit up when she said it, and Tori got the idea she was looking for an invitation. But Tori wasn't sure she wanted company. She almost thought she wanted to go alone and have some time with the baby. It didn't really make sense; the baby wasn't even born yet, and she was "alone" with him or her all the time. Maybe it was just because she was overwhelmed.

"That's okay. I'll get pictures and everything and show you, okay?"

"Okay. If that's what you want." Shelley smiled and reached for a cookie, but before she could take a bite, Tori blurted out the truth.

"Jeremy's in town."

Shelley dropped the cookie. It hit the coffee table and sugar sprinkled everywhere.

"*The* Jeremy? The father?"

She nodded and focused on her cup. "Yeah. He came on business and thought he'd look me up. And found me like this." She pointed to her stomach.

Shelley sat back on the sofa. "Oh, honey. Well, at least now he knows."

Tori looked up at her mom and grimaced. "Yeah. That decision was taken out of my hands."

"Maybe it's for the best. I know it's awkward, but I always thought he should know."

"I know. And me too, really. I'm just…scared."

"Scared that he'll what? Leave you alone? Not be supportive?"

On the contrary. Tori took another fortifying drink of tea. The other day, looking at houses, that kiss… All it had done was remind Tori of how much she'd enjoyed being with Jeremy in the first place. Yes, their relationship had been mostly physical over the summer. But she'd *liked* him…a lot. While she hadn't fostered any dreams of being whisked away to a fairy-tale ending, she had cherished their time together and had tucked the memories away as something very special. Her biggest fear was how to negotiate parenthood without letting her heart get involved. He was a good guy, underneath. He could have made things difficult for her, and instead he was taking his time, not making any demands. But for how long?

She was sure that at some point there was going to be a price to pay.

"You're quiet, so I guess there's more going on here than you want to talk to your mom about." Shelley's eyebrow lifted in a wry expression, but it wasn't condemning. They were close, but Tori had never really shared all the details with her mom.

"He's rich, Mom. Like lots-of-zeroes rich. And if he wanted to, he could make things really difficult."

"Do you think he would?" Concern overtook Shelley's face and her eyes darkened.

"I don't want to think so. He's nice. Caring, really. He hasn't made any demands. We're just… talking."

"Talking is good."

"He wants to be a part of the baby's life."

"That's good, isn't it? It shows he wants to step up. Be responsible."

"It also means I'll have to see him. And I wonder if he'll change his mind about how much custody he wants. If he decides that, I can't afford to challenge him. I'm scared, Mama." Her lips quivered a little on the last word; she rarely called her mom "Mama." "I love this baby already."

"Oh, honey, of course you do." Shelley moved over to the love seat where Tori sat. "You have to have faith, you know? You say he's a good man. I'm sure, then, that you can work this out."

"He is. We spent the day together on Thursday.

It was fun. He said if we are going to co-parent, we need to be able to spend time together."

"He's not wrong." Shelley looked at Tori a little more closely. "But is there more? I mean, there's a reason why you got pregnant. Is that still a factor?"

"I don't know." She let the words out on a breath. "Yeah, I still find him attractive, and there's still…something. At least for me. And I think for him, too. He…"

She halted. Swallowed against a lump in her throat. That kiss had been…something. More destructive to her defenses in its sweetness than any passionate overture might have been.

"He what, honey?"

"He kissed me under the lobby mistletoe."

Shelley laughed lightly. "Sweetie, you could do worse than kissing a good-looking millionaire in the lobby."

"Billionaire," she corrected. "Jeremy Fisher is a billionaire, thanks to his trust fund, his business, and apparently a sister who is a genius with stocks."

Shelley's mouth fell open. "Well."

"How do I prepare myself for this, Mom? I couldn't care less about his money, but it does change things. We live in different countries and are from different worlds. And we're having a kid together. It's such a mess."

Shelley reached for her hand and squeezed it. "You get through it just like you get through anything else. One day at a time, making the best decisions you know how. And then you trust everything will work out."

"You have a lot more faith than I do."

"I don't think so. Just keep an open mind. And if you do everything for the right reasons, chances are it's gonna be fine in the end." She let go of Tori's hand. "Now, have another cookie and drink your tea. Do you want to stay for dinner?"

"Of course I do."

"Good. Then I can send you home with pot-pie leftovers."

Jeremy switched the phone to the other ear as he sat at the table in his suite, his laptop open in front of him. "So it's down to the one on the river, or the one with the lighthouse, yeah?"

Branson's voice came over the line loud and clear. "I trust you, Jer. You know what I need right now."

His friend needed time and space. "I'm worried you'll become a long-haired, shaggy-bearded hermit who yells at kids to get off his lawn."

A rare, rusty laugh from Branson came over the line. "I don't like beards."

Which was true. But still, Jeremy worried.

"You're sure there's no place closer to the city? Or south, somewhere warm?"

"No one knows me up there. No one will recognize me. I need that for a while. And when the house outlives its purpose, I'll sell it again. No big."

"Then the lighthouse one. It's a better value, and to be honest, the location is spectacular enough it should move on resale within a reasonable time frame."

"Put in an offer. I'll pay the asking price. And a quick close."

"You're going to move north during the winter. Are you nuts?"

"I need to get out of here. The house is too full of ghosts."

Which was fair enough.

"Hey, Bran? Can I unload something on you for a minute?"

There was a pause. "Yeah, of course. I owe you a ton in therapy minutes."

They both chuckled a little. It wasn't like they kept score.

"So, remember the girl I told you about? From last summer?"

"Yeah, the fling. You said you were going to look her up again. How'd you make out?"

"She's pregnant."

When he said it all the air rushed out of his

lungs. It was almost like until this moment it wasn't really official. He hadn't told anyone until now. Because sometimes you needed your best buddy to give your head a whack.

"Nice work, Romeo. And she didn't tell you?"

"It's complicated."

"Well, duh." There was a pause. "So what now?"

"I don't know. I won't ignore my kid, you know? I can't do that."

"Of course not. And you're a good catch, you know. The electric bill will always be paid on time."

"I'm not sure she's ready for New York. And I'd be bored here within a month."

"So you split your time."

"I guess."

"Your mom know yet?"

"Hell, no."

"Well, my one piece of advice is if you consider making a play for this girl, you be up front with what your family is like before it's all settled. Don't blindside her with it after you've brokered a deal."

"Parenting isn't like buying a house."

Bran laughed again. "Good, I'm glad you came to that conclusion all on your own. Feel better?"

"Yes and no. But thank you. I'll be in touch about the offer."

"Just send me what I need to sign. I trust you."

They ended the call and Jeremy rested his forehead on his hands for a few moments. Bran was right. He needed Tori to meet his family. And he wanted to meet her mom, too.

What an unholy mess.

He made another call and verbally made an offer on the property. Considering he was offering asking price, he was relatively sure that it would be a simple transaction. Once that was done, he ventured down to the business center to take care of the necessary paperwork. As he was sending it off, he realized this meant he no longer had to be at the Sandpiper for more than a few more days. He could pack his things and head back to Manhattan. Get ready for Christmas.

It seemed odd and empty to think about now.

"So, did your friend decide on a house?"

He startled, jumping in his seat as her voice came from behind him.

"Sorry. I didn't mean to scare you."

"I was just thinking." He clicked his mouse and then looked up at her. She was glowing, dressed in black leggings and heels that accentuated her long legs, and a maternity top in a blue that matched the tartan on the Christmas tree. "You look good. Feeling well?"

"I slept a lot on the weekend and read a good book. It was heavenly."

She'd slept and he'd been doing some business in Halifax. They hadn't seen each other at all over the weekend. "I'm glad. And yes. Unless something falls through, it's the house in Kingsburg."

"The one with the lighthouse!" Her eyes lit up. "Oh, that's great. It's so impressive." Then she looked at him thoughtfully. "It does mean that you'll have a good friend in the area."

He hadn't actually considered that before. It was true. At least for a while, Bran would be here. She would be here, and their baby. He had ties to the South Shore without ever intending to.

"It also means I'll be leaving to go back to New York in a few days."

"I suppose it does."

Did she look disappointed? He almost hoped so. Plus they hadn't really come to any conclusions.

He wasn't sure quite what to say when her face changed and her hand went to the swell of her belly. "Whoa."

Alarm skittered through his veins as he shot up from the chair. "Are you all right? What's wrong?"

"Nothing." She looked up at him with wide eyes. "I think the baby just moved."

He guided her to the chair. "Really? What did it feel like?"

"I don't know. Like butterflies, kind of, but

running in a line down my belly. I've felt similar things lately, but not this strong. Oh, my, maybe the baby has been moving and I didn't know it!" Her face broke into a smile. "Oh, there it is again."

She reached for his hand and put it on her top, pressed against the solid curve. He didn't have time to react or hesitate; one moment he was standing there and the next he was crouched by her side, palm pressed against her navel. He waited, holding his breath, and then felt the tiniest flutter against his hand. "Is that it?"

She grinned and nodded. "You can feel it? I wasn't sure it would be strong enough."

It was. His child was in there, moving around, and his mother looked like a flipping angel, a perfect picture of motherhood. Something joyful and expansive filled his chest, while a balancing cold trickle of fear ran down his spine. This was amazing! And absolutely terrifying.

He waited, but there was no more movement, so he reluctantly took his hand away and stood again. She let out a huge breath, and then looked up into his face. "You okay? You've got a bit of a deer-in-the-headlights look about you."

"I'm all right. Terrified, but all right."

"I know. It takes some getting used to."

"It just got really real today, I think. I told my friend Branson, too."

She stood and went to him, putting her hand on his shoulder. "I've had a few months of pregnancy so I'm past the surreal part. You've got some catching up to do."

She'd gone through finding out and dealing with the first weeks alone, and an internet search had quickly told him what she'd probably gone through. He'd found out just yesterday that the baby was probably roughly the size of a banana now.

"Jeremy?" She called him back out of his thoughts. "I'm a bit late having my ultrasound, but it's scheduled for tomorrow afternoon. Do you want to go with me?"

Pictures of his baby. His! He felt as if he were being thrown into the deep end so very quickly, but he also knew there was really no other way. "I'd like that. A lot."

"It's in Bridgewater. Kind of close to that first house we saw last week."

"That's fine. You just tell me when we need to leave and I'll be ready."

"Okay." She reached down and took his hand. "It's going to be okay, you know. We'll figure everything out. My mom told me this weekend to have faith, and that's what I'm going to do."

Faith. Jeremy smiled but his heart wasn't in it. He didn't have faith. Not in anything, or really anyone. And Tori was making a mistake if she was placing her faith in him. He could try to live up to it, but chances were he'd fail. There was a reason that he was still single at thirty-six, and never been married. The women who liked him, he didn't like in return. And the ones he liked, he didn't trust. The guys were right. He was a serial dater. It kept him from being lonely, without the messiness of emotions and expectations.

He liked Tori, liked her too much. And he wanted to trust her. But faith? That was just asking for trouble.

Tori had thought what she wanted was to go to the ultrasound alone, but as she sat in the waiting room with Jeremy, she was glad she wasn't alone. And that he was there. He was the baby's father, after all. It seemed right that they share this moment together.

"Are you nervous?"

She looked over at him. His knee bounced up and down. "I think you're the nervous one."

He stopped bouncing his knee and smiled sheepishly. "It feels weird. I never imagined I'd be a father."

"Really? You never wanted a family?" She appreciated how well he'd accepted the situation, and his promises to be there, but it worried her that he might not have seen this role as part of his future.

"It wasn't so much wanting or not wanting," he revealed. "It's more… I just didn't have a great example to follow, and believe it or not, dating is hard with my money."

She gave the obligatory laugh, but then put her hand on his knee. "It must be hard to figure out who's genuine and who's after your bank account. I don't have that problem." And then she laughed again. And hoped he realized she didn't care about his money, either.

"Yeah, there's that. Some women want the status. But I have my own issues. I don't trust easily. Other people, or my own intuition. When it comes to relationships, anyway."

"Then this situation must be driving you crazy," she said, jostling his shoulder. "Because now there's a baby mama in the mix."

"You're being awfully chill about this."

She shrugged. "I am what I am. I can't make you believe that I'm genuine, that I don't want your money or that I'm out for anything. All I can do is tell you my truth. You're the father. I can and will do this by myself if you bail. I can support me and my child, and I'll be okay. So there's no pressure from me on your bank account. Just room for you to be a father."

She turned sideways in her chair and met his gaze squarely. "My only demand is that if you choose to be involved, you're consistent and hon-

want our kid always to be wondering
er coming back or if you care."

To her surprise, his eyes softened. "I *was* that kid, Tori. I won't do that to my own." He swallowed and his throat bobbed with the effort. "I promise you I will not be that dad."

"Then we will figure everything else out."

The door across from them opened. "Victoria? We're ready for you now."

They went in together. Jeremy waited to the side while Tori got on the bed with the paper sheet beneath her. The room was warm, thankfully, and in a few moments they'd adjusted her clothing so that her shirt was up and the waistbands of her leggings and underwear were rolled down right to her pubic bone. She looked over at Jeremy and realized his eyes had widened, looking at her belly. He hadn't seen it before, not like this. She smiled up at him, reassuringly. "You gonna be okay, Dad?" she asked lightly.

He nodded. "Yeah. Yeah."

"Okay, then," the technician said. "Let's get started." She squirted gel on Tori's belly, then began, the pressure from the probe firm. Tori couldn't see the screen, though she wouldn't know what she was looking at anyway. The tech made clicks here and there, saying that she was taking measurements first. Then she turned the screen around. "Okay, are you ready to see?"

During Tori's first scan, at only eight weeks, there'd been very little to see. This time, however, was different. The image shifted, but she could make out the head, and the ridge that was the spine, and appendages. "Look at the little toes," she whispered, tears forming in the corners of her eyes.

She tore her gaze away to look at Jeremy, who was staring at the screen in wonder. "That's our baby. My kid." His fingers flexed and unflexed. "I just… I can't…"

"Do you want to know what you're having? I can't tell you today, but the report will go to your doctor."

Tori looked up at him. "I don't mind it being a surprise. Gender's not important to me anyway." Her only concern was that the baby be healthy. Besides, she didn't go into all the pink and blue stuff and gender-reveal things. She'd already started decorating her tiny second bedroom with a Beatrix Potter theme, something neutral. Peter Rabbit and Squirrel Nutkin were way too cute.

"If you want it to be a surprise, then that's fine with me," he said.

"You're sure?"

"Whatever you want." A smile broke out over his face. "Wow. That's our kid in there."

It was the genuine smile that did it. He'd moved past the looks of alarm and panic to that of…

Well, looking at him right now all she could see was joy. Relief swamped her heart as well as a feeling of…happiness? Was that possible? Their relationship was still something they didn't talk about. Nothing had been decided about how they were going to make this work. But she remembered what her mom had said only a few days earlier. One day at a time. And today she was going to enjoy this lovely moment.

"Do you want to see the heartbeat?" the tech asked.

"Yes." There was no hesitation from Jeremy and Tori laughed.

She pointed to a spot on the screen where the *ba-bump*, *ba-bump* flash flickered in a little heart.

Jeremy went around to the foot of the bed and sat, covering his mouth with a hand. Tori watched him as he stared at the monitor, feeling her heart slipping bit by bit. He said he didn't trust. He'd had a loveless childhood, from the sounds of it. And yet he was capable of so much feeling. He was good, underneath it all. She truly believed that. Could she keep her feelings for him under wraps? Wait it out until they faded? Wasn't it natural to have feelings about the father of her baby?

Even if they weren't returned…or couldn't lead anywhere?

She looked back at the monitor again, and the form of her unborn child there. Every decision she made had to be for the good of her baby. They were the most important thing now.

"Okay, give me a few minutes and I'll take some pictures for you." The tech started moving the wand again, then held it in position and hit a few keys. She tried again and started to chuckle. "Your baby's moving around in there and won't sit still. So much for napping."

It took another few minutes but then it was done and the tech gave her a towel to wipe away the gel as the pictures printed. "I'll give you a few minutes to put yourself back together." She handed the pictures to Jeremy. "Congratulations."

Tori wiped off the gel and adjusted her clothing, then got up from the bed and dropped the cloth in the used bin. When she returned, she stopped in front of Jeremy. "Are you okay?"

He nodded. "I think so." He reached out and pulled her closer, so his hand was on her hip and his face was just below her breasts. He cradled her bump and then, to her surprise, placed a kiss on it. Tears stung her eyes at the tender gesture.

"Are you real?" she asked softly, putting her hands on each side of his head. He looked up and into her eyes. "You could have run the moment you found out. You could have offered to buy me off. You could have made demands. But you haven't, and I don't understand, and I'm… I'm afraid that someday soon there's going to be a price I need to pay and I don't know what it is."

He sighed, a heavy, weighted sigh that sounded so weary she wasn't quite sure what to say.

"I'm trying to do the right thing," he finally said. "I'm as responsible for this as you are. There is no blame and if there is, we share it equally. The truth is, that's my child in there. I saw them on the screen and saw their heart beating. It's humbling, Tori. I have no idea how to do this but I want us to try."

"Us," she said, a bit numb from what she thought he might mean.

"We're going to be parents together. We like each other. For God's sake, we kissed the other day."

"You kissed me," she clarified, though her heart thumped against her ribs.

He stood then, so she had to look up the tiniest bit. "If you tell me there's nothing between us at all, I'll drop the subject right now. But if there is, don't we owe it to our baby to try?"

"If we blow it, the stakes are really high," she responded. And yet he was so close she could smell his cologne and feel his warmth. She couldn't lie and say there was nothing between them because there was. Both the attraction from the summer, and the depth of character he'd shown since his return. He'd been far more understanding than a lot of men might have been.

"Look. Look at this picture and tell me this little nugget doesn't deserve us to try at the very least."

She hesitated but couldn't take her eyes off the ultrasound picture. And he'd called him or her a nugget. It was an adorable little name.

Jeremy cupped her cheek, then kissed her forehead. "Let me take you home. Maybe we can talk it over."

Her home. Where she had, in all likelihood, conceived their child. Where they'd spent lazy evenings after a day at the beach. And lazy morning-afters, watching the sunrise.

"Okay," she replied. "Let's go home. And talk."

Because she was really unsure about this step, and they needed to set some solid boundaries.

CHAPTER SEVEN

SHE WAS VERY aware of how small her house was when they stepped in it again, Jeremy for the first time since last July. Just under a thousand square feet meant two bedrooms, a small kitchen with dining area to the side, a modest living room and a bathroom that was smaller than the closet in his suite at the Sandpiper. Still, it suited her well. It was cozy, and it was hers.

He didn't seem to mind as he removed his coat and draped it over the back of her sofa. He slipped off his shoes, too, and left them by the door, stepping inside in his socks. Today he'd worn jeans and a simple sweater, and the look of him in casual clothing, so approachable, made her want to slip into his arms. But she couldn't. Not with what he'd suggested hovering between them.

Could they be more than simple co-parents? More than…friends?

"You're nervous," he said quietly, moving toward her. "Don't be."

"How can I not?" She turned around, fold-

ing her hands in front of her. "What you said...
It would change everything. I was thinking we
could just be friends. Work together as a team.
But not..."

Her voice trailed off.

"Not lovers?" he answered, reaching out and
putting his hand along her upper arm, rubbing
gently.

"Yes, that," she answered, trying hard to keep
her breath even. Right now, despite the thread
of desire winding its way through her body, she
couldn't imagine having sex with him. Her body
had changed. Heck, everything had changed. It
certainly wouldn't be a summer fling.

He gazed into her eyes for a long moment, then
leaned closer, slowly, giving her lots of time to
move away, or put a hand on his chest to stop
him, or say no. But she couldn't, because the
truth was she wanted him to kiss her. Wanted to
feel his lips on hers again. His arms around her
without mistletoe overhead or staff meters away.

He touched his lips to hers, and she let out a
breath. More of a sigh, really, as his arms came
around her and pulled her close. Her mouth
opened beneath his and she let him guide her,
softly, seductively, no rush. Like they had all the
time in the world.

She melted against his chest and tilted her head
up a bit, hungry for more. Her wordless request

was rewarded with a deeper kiss, more urgency, and the desire that had been a slow burn began to blaze brighter.

This was what had gotten them into this mess in the first place. Not that her baby would ever be a "mess," but the situation was certainly complicated.

She pulled back a bit, startled by her response to him, needing space to breathe and think.

"I, uh…" That was as far as she got. Actual words weren't making it from her brain to her mouth.

"I know. It's not what we expected. Well, actually, it is what I expected when I came back. That we could go out again, have some fun. I think it's clear that the attraction is still alive and well. We can't ignore it, you know? Because it'll crop up from time to time."

"I can't deny that, after what just happened." She moved another step backward. His unflinching tendency to state the obvious was at times refreshing and other times vastly uncomfortable. He liked to deal with problems head-on. She did, too, or so she had thought. Still, highlighting the fact that there was still sexual attraction simmering between them threw her off balance. It wasn't something they could compartmentalize in a little box, isolated from the situation.

The sad bit of it was, she wanted him to kiss

her again, and again, until her head was swimming with it, and the scent of his cologne, and the feel of his hands on her… Being pregnant hadn't eradicated her libido. Actually, in this moment, she wondered if it hadn't increased. She crossed her arms in front of her and tried to ignore the sensations running through her body.

"We're having a child," she said, and wondered how many times over the last week she'd said those words. "Where do you see this going? Because we're going to be tied together for life, do you understand that? If this goes sideways, it could be a disaster."

But if it didn't…

A secret want bubbled up in her. What would it be like for them to be a family? The two of them together, their child…more children? She gave herself a mental shake. How would that even work? Once again she reminded herself they were from two very different worlds. That the fairy tale had never been in the equation.

"You think we need to set boundaries. Figure out the what-ifs."

"Yes," she said, letting out a huge breath of relief. "That's it exactly."

He went to her, took her hand and led her to the sofa. "Come, sit down. I don't like the idea of us staring each other down like we're in a negotiation."

She followed him and sank into the sofa, the cushions cradling her lower back, which had started to bother her a little after the long day.

"You want to know what happens if we try this and one of us walks away. From a romantic relationship," he clarified. "Not parenthood. We both agree we're in that for the long haul."

"Yes. And there are a lot of things to figure out. I live here. You live in New York. How would it work?"

"I actually have an idea about that," he said, reaching for her hand. He turned on the sofa a bit and tucked his left ankle under his right leg, so he was facing her. "Come to New York with me for a week."

Her stomach plummeted. "A week? In December? Before Christmas?"

He nodded, undaunted. "Yeah. Christmas in New York is amazing. I can show you the sights… Have you ever been?"

She shook her head. She really hadn't traveled much of anywhere. One year, in high school, they'd taken the CAT ferry from Yarmouth to Bar Harbor and gone to Old Orchard Beach. The rest of her travel had been east of Toronto.

Jeremy squeezed her fingers. "I'll take some time off. We can spend it together, figuring things out. With no one interfering."

So this wasn't a ploy to convince her to move

there, but to give them time away to evaluate? She sighed. "I don't know…" She pulled away a bit, feeling incredibly overwhelmed with it all. "Jeremy, a week ago I hadn't even decided how and when to tell you, and now you're here, and we're trying to sort out how we're going to do this, and you've kissed me…twice…"

"And you kissed me back," he said firmly. "If it's boundaries you're worried about, then let me put it plainly for you. If for any reason something…more…comes of this, but then either one of us wants to pull the plug, then we can. With the important thing being we do so amicably with the well-being of the baby first and foremost."

It sounded so simple and logical when he put it that way. Could it really be that easy?

Her heart—and her head—said no.

And yet the man sitting next to her, with the earnest eyes and seriously kissable lips, made her believe yes. The idea of a whole week in New York was enticing. She'd only ever seen videos and pictures of things like the giant Christmas tree in Rockefeller Square, the shops on Fifth Avenue…

"I don't know, Jeremy," she whispered. "This—all of this—is so crazy and scary. Everything about my life is changing. Now, talking about going away for a week, together…"

She bit down on her lip. "I'm finding it hard to keep up."

He lifted his hand and put it along her cheek. "Don't worry. We'll use it as get-to-know-each-other time. No pressure. No decisions. You're right about one thing. Last summer was so fast, and now we're being thrust into parenthood. If we stand any chance of doing this together, we have to know each other better. Develop trust. I know where you live and your world. But you don't know mine."

It all sounded perfect, which was exactly why Tori was so uneasy. Nothing was ever perfect.

"I'll have to ask for the time off first," she said, surprised she was actually considering it.

"We can go whenever you like. I can work my schedule around you, though I do have a series of meetings on the nineteenth and twentieth I can't miss."

"So I'd be back here for Christmas."

"I'm sure you'll want to be with your mom, won't you?"

She nodded. "Okay. I'll go."

A wide smile lit up his face. "That's great!" He gathered her hands in his and kissed her knuckles. "We're going to be fine. Just wait and see."

Jeremy watched as Tori's eyes widened at the sight of the private jet sitting on the tarmac at

Halifax's airport. The option for a direct flight would have taken them only to Newark, with all the other flights requiring a stop. Why would he do that when he could charter something and leave on his own schedule?

Plus he wasn't above trying to impress her a little bit. The woman deserved a bit of pampering and glamour. She worked hard and didn't have a lot to show for it. A cozy little house, sure, and a close-knit work family. But there was a big world out there and he wanted to show her a little bit of it.

"Is this yours?"

He laughed. "No. I chartered it."

Her face relaxed. "Oh. I was having a moment thinking you had your own plane and I was... I don't know."

"I thought about it, and went back and forth about whether I wanted to own one, but in the end, I keep coming back to using charters. It seemed simpler than worrying about where to keep it, having a pilot on call, maintenance... This way I pick up the phone, my assistant books me a charter and I show up." He took her arm as they got to the steps leading to the door. "I like to keep things simple, believe it or not."

It was her turn to laugh. "Jeremy, there is nothing simple about you."

He wasn't sure if that was a compliment or

a criticism, but her voice was easy and a smile was on her lips so he was going to take it as a compliment.

She climbed the stairs ahead of him. He watched the gentle sway of her hips, thinking how pretty she looked in jeans and ankle boots with her jacket bundled up around her. She turned and flashed a smile at him when she reached the door and he realized he loved how young and energetic she looked with her hair back in a simple perky ponytail and the minimal makeup she wore, which made her skin look fresh and dewy. Or maybe that was her pregnant glow. It was then that he noticed how snug the jacket was around her tummy. She was only going to get bigger, and the winter was barely begun.

A shopping trip would definitely be on the itinerary.

Once inside, an attendant named Gerry took their coats and got them settled in soft leather seats. The more Tori looked around, the happier Jeremy was that he'd booked the flight. Her lips were open in what he thought was amazement and her eyes flitted over every seat, table and detail of decor in the Gulfstream.

They took off, and her face was fairly stuck to the window as they raced down the runway and left solid ground beneath them.

"This is maybe the coolest thing I've ever

done," she said, turning away and smiling up at him. "Is this normal for you? I don't know how I'd ever get used to it."

"It wasn't always. For a while I usually booked first class." He grinned at her. "And some of the commuter jets don't even have a first class." He shuddered for effect, making her laugh.

"I'd be disappointed if I thought you meant that," she replied, sitting back against the comfortable seat. "But you aren't the pretentious type. At least, I don't think you are."

He frowned a little. "That's one of the reasons I suggested the week, Tori. So we could get to know each other better. But I'm relieved you don't think I'm a stuck-up snob."

"Stuck up, no. Used to the finer things? Definitely."

At that moment, Gerry returned. "Are you ready for your breakfast, sir?"

"Breakfast?" Tori parroted, looking from Jeremy to Gerry and back again.

"You didn't think I wasn't going to feed you, did you? It's only ten. If you ate at all this morning, it was hours ago." It was true, because it was over two hours to the airport, and they'd had to return his rental to the agency, then clear security and then customs before boarding.

The meal smelled delicious, and Gerry whisked the cover away to reveal scrambled eggs, a bagel with butter and jam, and heaps of fresh strawberries and raspberries. "Would you like something to drink, ma'am?" he asked.

"Oh, goodness." The low rumble of her stomach was audible, and Jeremy hid a smile. "Maybe some orange juice? Or even just iced water would be lovely."

He took Jeremy's lid as well and Jeremy said, "Water is fine for me, thank you, Gerry."

"This is too much," she said when Gerry had disappeared.

"It's scrambled eggs," Jeremy laughed. "I mean, it's not like it's eggs Benedict or anything elaborate. But I do know that you like eggs in the morning."

Her eyes widened. "You do?"

"You mentioned it one morning when I first arrived. You said Neil made them just the way you liked."

He watched as she took a bite and then turned her amazed gaze to him. "With a bit of cheese and some parsley. I can't believe you remembered that."

The approval in her gaze made him go all warm inside. "Well, I'll confess I asked Neil. Because I get the feeling that you'll just go along with anything rather than voice any preferences."

She put her fork down and her face sobered,

her lips turning downward. "What's wrong? Did I say something?" he asked.

"You're half right. I probably would be happy to just go along with things. But maybe I pick my battles. Scrambled eggs, no big deal. Our child's future…big deal."

She wasn't going to be a pushover. Good. Not that he didn't want to get his way, but he admired strength. "Of course."

Gerry returned with orange juice and water for Tori and water for Jeremy, and left quietly. They ate their breakfast in companionable silence, until Tori sat back with a satisfied sigh. "Okay, so you were right. That was delicious and I needed the protein. Thank you."

"You're most welcome. What would you like to do today? We'll be at my place before noon."

"I have no idea." She laughed. "I guess I figured you'd have an itinerary."

"Sometimes the best vacations don't have itineraries," he replied, and cocked an eyebrow.

She blushed prettily. The last "vacation" for both of them had been those magical days in the summer, when they'd soaked up the sun and each other, with no schedule whatsoever. "Jeremy, if you're expecting…" She swallowed and her blush deepened.

"I have no expectations beyond wanting to show you my town," he replied, then reached over to take her hand. His heart hammered in his chest. There was no denying that the attraction to her hadn't gone away. But it was something he wanted to work with, not against. To acknowledge, not ignore. "You're a beautiful woman, Tori. I'm not going to lie and say that what I'm feeling is totally platonic. But I'm not going to push."

Her eyes delved into his. "Me, too," she breathed. "And I shouldn't have admitted that, I suppose. I'm not good at holding my cards close to my chest."

"This isn't poker, or some business merger. It's okay. I'm glad you're being honest."

"Me, too. About you, I mean."

The statement left him somewhat uncomfortable, because he hadn't been completely honest with her about what he really wanted. He was more…hoping she'd come around to the same way of thinking without him having to say so. He wanted her to love his place, love New York and to want to be closer. Hell, he'd even consider living somewhere else and commuting. He was saved from saying more as Gerry returned to take their plates away, bring Jeremy fresh coffee and put a tiny pot of steaming water and a cup in front of Tori.

She looked up in confusion and he smiled at her. "Mint tea, ma'am. Mr. Fisher said you preferred it."

"Thank you, Gerry."

She looked over at Jeremy and raised an eyebrow. "Well, aren't you one for anticipating my needs," she said, a hint of sarcasm in her voice.

"Too much?" he asked, sitting back in his seat. He loved it when she had a hint of sass, and his lips twitched.

"I could tell you it's a bit obvious. Or perhaps heavy-handed. But it smells heavenly." She poured from the pot into her cup and the refreshing scent of mint filled the air. "So I should probably just say thank you."

He leaned forward, determined to be honest, at least in the moment. "No, thank you. For coming on this trip. For being so open-minded and for not pushing back when I said I wanted to be a part of our baby's life."

"You're the father," she said simply.

"Yes, but I know you didn't have to tell me, and considered not doing so. I arrived and took that decision out of your hands, and I'm not sorry. But I know it's been difficult and I appreciate you meeting me in the middle."

More than that. He wanted to treat her well because seeing her walk through those grand houses had made him see that he wanted to be able to convince her to be closer. He didn't want to have to fly every few months to see his kid. He couldn't run his business from Back-End-of-No-where, Nova Scotia, either. Dictating his desires would accomplish nothing; the right way was to make her want this for herself. His wonderful home in Manhattan. Top schools and opportunities. Weekends away, and no financial stress. In exchange, he'd be there for his kid—the one thing in the world he wanted most. He would never be an absentee father like his own dad had been. His child would never have to wonder if he was loved or if his father even cared at all.

Seeing the ultrasound picture that now lay tucked in his wallet, remembering the steady flicker of the heartbeat on the monitor as they watched... That had changed everything. As had feeling him or her kick against his hand. It had turned an idea into something utterly tangible.

"Likewise," she responded, her gaze soft. "You've been so understanding. Way more than I gave you credit for. I should have told you from the beginning."

"It doesn't matter. It really doesn't. Let's just keep looking forward."

"Deal." She took a sip of tea, then looked out the window for a few moments before turning back to him. "And what about...well...us?"

It was a tough question. He couldn't lie and say he was in love with her. He wasn't. They got along well and enjoyed being together, didn't they? And there was attraction on both sides.

There was certainly more warmth between them than had ever been between his parents, obviously, or his mom and stepdad. He wasn't sure he even believed in a burning passion that lasted forever. Hell, his brother was an aficionado of everlasting love and had believed in it so strongly he'd tried it…three times.

So he was as honest as he dared to be. "Tori, you're beautiful, and smart, and you make me laugh. You have this way of lifting one eyebrow that literally makes me hear you say 'Really, Jeremy?' in my mind. You light up when you talk about the baby. Your staff loves you and you love them… And that doesn't often happen with management. It wasn't an accident we connected last summer. And all the things I liked about you then I still like about you now."

She twisted her hands in her lap, as if his declaration made her uncomfortable. She gave an odd laugh and shrugged. "The things you liked about me then? I'm afraid I definitely don't look as good in a bikini as I did last summer."

He remembered, all right. She'd had a red one that seemed to be held together by strings, and then a black one that tied around her neck and made her breasts look—

He clenched his jaw. The image that flooded his brain now was of her in that same bikini, only with the gentle swell of their child curving her stomach. It was no less sexy in his mind.

"I'm not sure about that."

"Oh, I am. My boobs are bigger and wouldn't even fit in those cups—"

"I'm not seeing the problem here."

She stared at him, and then started to giggle. "Oh, I suppose not. But thanks for the laugh."

He wasn't exactly laughing. In fact, he had to shift in his seat to be a little more comfortable.

Gerry reappeared. "Sir, we're going to start our descent soon. In another five minutes or so, you'll need to fasten your seat belts."

"So soon?" Tori looked up with a smile. "Thank you. I think I'll freshen up before I have to get buckled in."

She rose from her seat and made her way to the bathroom. Jeremy ran his finger over his lower lip and tried to get the image of Tori in her bikini out of his mind, but he couldn't.

They'd shared a few relatively chaste kisses in the last week, but clearly the summer had been a lot more heated; the pregnancy was evidence enough of that. He had to admit to himself, at least, that he'd wondered about a sexual relationship with her again. They'd been incredibly compatible...

The more he thought about it, the more he realized that she was near perfect for him. Kind, funny, sexually compatible, she'd be a great mother. Smart and intuitive…there really wasn't anything he didn't like about her.

She checked all his boxes, and a few he hadn't realized he had.

When she returned from the bathroom, he smiled and waited for her to resume her seat and get buckled in. Then, as they approached, he pointed out landmarks through the window, half watching the view and half watching her.

That was it. He'd pull out all the stops. And make her see how perfect their life could be. Her, him and, most important of all, their baby.

CHAPTER EIGHT

TORI'S FIRST IMPRESSION of New York was of noise and traffic. She'd never seen anything like it, and on the drive from La Guardia to the Upper East Side, she'd basically kept her nose pressed against the window of the luxury car that had been waiting for them when they arrived. Not a stretch limo or anything, thank goodness, but a bona fide car service and driver. *Surreal* didn't even begin to cover what she'd already experienced today.

They were dropped off outside Jeremy's building. It didn't look like anything overly special from the outside, but inside was a different story. They took an elevator to his floor, and when he opened the door to his home, she nearly gasped.

What she did immediately was remove her leather boots and place them by the door. There was no way she would track on these floors.

The floor of the foyer gleamed like glass, and just beyond was a kitchen to the left. White cupboards, stainless state-of-the-art appliances, a slate-gray butcher block in the center and an enormous bouquet of fresh flowers made it look more like one of his real estate showings than a home. The concept was open, but a partial wall separated the working part of the kitchen—which looked as if it had never been used—from a dining room. A long table with upholstered chairs was the centerpiece of the space, with a long, silver runner down the middle and a bowl of more flowers sitting in its center. The table had seating for eight, and Tori could almost imagine a dinner party around such a table, with the clink of silverware and tinkle of crystal.

Yep. Definitely out of her league.

"Over here is the living room," Jeremy said from behind her, and she turned to see him holding out an arm. She followed close behind and was bathed in sunlight from the windows. "You can see the park from here," he offered, taking her hand and pulling her forward. She looked out the window... Indeed, there was lots of city around them, but also the huge expanse of Central Park, now covered with an inch of snow, looking cold but a little magical, too.

She was no Realtor but she knew that location was everything. And that he had paid a lot of money for this particular location. She'd looked up his address on the internet, looked at a street view. He was close to the Met, to Central Park, Broadway...

It was nearly overwhelming.

"What do you think?"

She turned to face him and found his face expectant. She glanced around at the impeccably decorated living room. To be honest, it was beautiful but it was missing something. It seriously felt like one of his listings, staged for a potential buyer, made to look wonderful without revealing the personality of the person who lived within.

There wasn't much of Jeremy here. But clearly he was proud of it, so she smiled. "It's gorgeous."

His answering grin made her glad she'd answered as she did. "Come on, let me show you the rest."

The rest included a powder room, plus two more full bathrooms—one main bathroom between two bedrooms and then a luxurious en suite bathroom off the master. The guest rooms were impeccable, of course, and the master bedroom housed a king-size bed with a black leather headboard and a thick silver duvet. The top was turned down to reveal the ends of the sheets beneath, and they were black silk. Chrome-and-black bedside tables held a docking station for electronics and a lamp, and he pulled the drapes aside to reveal another breathtaking view.

He looked at her and smiled again. Were they going to smile their way through the next week?

"Whichever bedroom you'd like as yours is fine. The other bathroom is yours, as well."

At least he didn't assume they'd be sharing a room. Not that she'd expected that, but she'd gotten a little nervous on the plane after his bikini comment. As much as the idea of him still finding her attractive was exciting, she needed space and time to figure out if they truly could move forward as a couple. It felt like they kept taking steps that way, and then retreated into the safety of a relationship of utility and co-parenting.

Neither bedroom was overly welcoming. Beautiful, yes, but not…warm. That was it. The grayscale was trendy and definitely classy and elegant, but it was missing warmth.

"The one across the hall will be fine." She knew it had a queen-size bed and the bedding looked thicker and softer there. Like something she could curl up in.

"Great." He clapped his hands together. "I'll put your bag in your room so you can unpack. And then maybe we can go for a walk in the park."

A walk in the park was the perfect way to spend the afternoon. The air was crisp without being frigid, the sky a clear blue, and Jeremy reached down and held her hand as they wandered along. When she said she wanted a hot dog from a street vendor, he obliged, and they sat on a cold bench with cold noses, biting into hot dogs with sweet ketchup and sharp mustard. They wound their way around the paths and he showed her The Plaza, and she told him about one of her favorite children's book characters, Eloise. They had coffee in a little shop to warm their toes and fingers, and then when she looked longingly at the horse-drawn carriages, he obliged and they went on a carriage ride, which he said was eye-rollingly touristy but didn't complain when she got cold and leaned against him, prompting him to put his arm around her and cuddle her close.

The afternoon darkened and it was time to go home. It had been a marvelous first introduction to the Big Apple, and when Jeremy suggested she take a nap before dinner, she didn't put up any fight. She'd been up since five and the fresh air and walking had done its work.

After an hour he woke her and said that dinner was ready. He didn't let her in the kitchen, but seated her at the dining table, where he'd put two place settings at corners to each other, and lit a couple of candles. "Did you have a good nap?"

"The best. I woke up and forgot where I was."

He chuckled. "It's the fresh air. Plus you were up super early this morning."

"And I nap very easily these days," she admitted. "This growing-another-human thing takes some energy."

He disappeared into the kitchen and returned with a plate. "Which is why you need this. You've only had a hot dog and a latte since this morning."

The meal was simple. Chicken, asparagus and pasta were tossed in a white sauce, with a green salad on the side. But it was delicious and Tori ate up every bite on her plate.

"You're a decent cook. Where did you learn?"

"I can't take the credit. I eat out a lot and I have a housekeeper come in once a week. She also brings in a variety of meals and puts them in the fridge with instructions for reheating. I literally just had to put this in the oven, and voilà."

"Oh. Well, my compliments to the chef, whoever she may be." Jeremy was not the domestic type. It was more and more obvious as the day wore on. His apartment...condo...whatever barely looked lived in. There certainly weren't bits that jumped out as being "Jeremy." But he'd fed her and it had been scrumptious, so she patted her belly and said, "There. The baby's happy."

"Is he?" Jeremy's gaze met hers and held. "Is he happy?"

"Maybe it's a she."

"Of course. How about...are they happy?"

"I think so. At least it seems as if they're doing a jig in there."

His gaze deepened, and she thought she caught a glimpse of vulnerability. "May I feel?"

It was sweet of him to ask, lovely of him to want to. "Of course," she replied. She pushed her chair out a little, and so did he, and then slid to the edge of his seat so they bumped knees. He put his hand on her belly, his palm wide and warm. But the ripple of feeling was in a different spot, so she put her hand on his wrist and guided him to the left a little. Whether it was arms or legs or somersaults, it didn't take long and the movement thudded against his hand, little taps and rolls.

"Wow," he breathed, staring at his hand, then up at her. "I can't get over that. How does it feel, you know, on the inside?"

She knew he meant the actual sensation rather than her response, but all she could say was, "Wonderful."

He didn't move his hand. But he leaned forward and pressed his forehead to hers. Not kissing, just…connecting. Tears stung her eyes. Maybe this was what had drawn her to him in the first place. Connection. She'd had friends, coworkers. Her mom. But not this kind of connection with another human. Not for a very long time, because she'd always backed away, not trusting that she wouldn't be hurt or duped in the end, as she had been before.

And she'd never had a connection of this depth, because this time they shared a child. His DNA and hers had come together to create a whole other person. It was a huge and sobering thought.

"Jeremy," she whispered. Her throat swelled with unshed tears.

He leaned back and took his hand from her belly and rested it on her cheek. "I don't understand," he whispered back. "You already love this baby so much, and it isn't even born yet. And I don't—" His voice broke off, and he cleared his throat. "Damn, I'm not a little kid. I don't know why this gets to me. I just don't ever remember feeling this much warmth in my home."

Her heart broke a little. "Were there never any fun times? Laughter?"

He shrugged. "I suppose there must have been, but I don't really remember them much. Mom and Dad divorced before I really formed any solid memories. When we were little Mom and Bruce took us to Disney once. And we went to summer camps and that was fun. But I can't remember a single other family vacation that we took together. Mom and Bruce would take off for a weekend in the city, see a show, dinner, hotel. They definitely traveled while we were in school. But never with us."

It was impossible to fathom. "But who cared for you?"

His hand slipped away. "We had staff."

"Shut up! Are you serious?"

She looked so disgusted a smile turned up the corners of his mouth. "It wasn't so bad. Some of the nannies were okay, and I really got along with the gardener who came twice a week."

He had to have been so lonely…and felt so unloved. Her heart ached for the kind of boy he must have been. "That's horrible. And I'm amazed you turned out to be a decent human being, which I know you are, because you've been nothing but kind and understanding throughout this whole thing."

"If I am, it's only because of Merrick. I met my best friends there. Teachers who, for the most part, cared enough to turn us from spoiled, scared brats into actual humans. Not that it always worked, mind you." He chuckled softly. "As a group we were a rich, entitled bunch."

"Materially, maybe."

"I can't complain, Tori. I have had advantages that most people only dream of."

She was glad he realized it, but deep down she knew all the money in the world couldn't buy real affection and love. She thought of all the summers she'd gone camping with her parents to any of the provincial parks. They'd always allowed her to take a friend. There'd been swimming and playgrounds and campfires with roasted marshmallows that scalded the roof of her mouth. Christmases watching movies and drinking hot chocolate. They hadn't had a lot of money but they'd gone on a walk every Thanksgiving Day since she was a little girl, enjoying the fall weather and colors. There had been story time at night before bed, and when she was sick, her dad carrying her to her room and tucking her into bed. There hadn't always been a lot of money, but she wouldn't trade a single moment of it.

Jeremy didn't know anything about any of those things. Not through any fault of his own, but she wondered how he was going to handle a different kind of parenthood.

It worried her, but she wasn't about to deny him the opportunity to try.

She squeezed his fingers in hers. "It's gonna be okay. I'll help you. I had a great dad." Grief at his loss welled up, but gratitude, too, that he'd been a wonderful father. "I'll share him with you, tell you all about him and the stuff he used to do with me. You don't have to wait for the baby to be born to be a good father, Jeremy. You're doing it already."

His gaze snapped up to hers. "How come you are so great? Why aren't you scared? Freaking out about what's to come?"

"You think I'm not scared? Of course I am.

But deep down I believe everything is going to be okay. It has to be."

Faith. It seemed she had some after all.

He squeezed her fingers back. "Okay. I'm going to trust you. At least for now." Clearing his throat, he gave her fingers a final squeeze and then sat up straight. "What do you say we clean up these dishes and then watch a movie or something?"

"That sounds amazing."

The sky was dark but lit by the millions of city lights. After they loaded the dishwasher, Jeremy put down the blinds over the windows while Tori sank into the couch. It wasn't just for looks; the cushions were super comfortable and Jeremy came back with a soft throw blanket from a closet somewhere. "Okay, so regular movie or Christmas movie?"

She was in Manhattan in December. "Christmas, and *Miracle on 34th Street*."

He laughed. "When in Rome… So, original or remake?" He handed her the blanket and reached for his phone. She shook her head. He could control everything from that thing.

"I know I should say the original…but the remake. Because Richard Attenborough *is* Santa Claus."

"Yes, but Natalie Wood…"

"I know. So my pick tonight, yours tomorrow?"

"Sounds fair."

He scrolled through a streaming app until he found the movie, and then it was on, complete with Thanksgiving Day parade, a drunk parade Santa and Mara Wilson looking adorable. Halfway through he disappeared to make her a cup of tea—apparently said housekeeper had stocked up on a few things before their arrival—and after sipping at the comforting brew, Tori found herself blinking slowly.

She shouldn't be tired. She'd had a wonderful nap before dinner.

Jeremy shifted on the sofa. "Here. Lean against me. You'll be more comfortable and have some support for your neck."

He lifted his arm and she curled in against his side, the soft blanket covering her from waist to toes. He was so warm and stable, and her belly rested against his hip as if it were perfectly suited for the angle. And oh, he smelled good. Like clean clothes and the expensive cologne he always wore. She closed her eyes and inhaled.

On the screen, Dylan McDermott was proposing to Elizabeth Perkins, a huge ring in a red box. Tori opened her eyes and sighed.

"What?"

"I never understand why she's so mean to Bryan in this moment."

"Well, she's afraid."

"I know that. But it makes her stupid."

Jeremy chuckled, low in his chest. "Then there's the fact that there's still a lot of movie to get through and the happy ending. Why would people keep watching if she said yes?"

She looked up at him. "To see if Kris Kringle is real, of course."

He shook his head. "Uh-uh. You know as well as I do that the love story is the main attraction here. And the question of whether or not Susan gets her house and a dad and a baby brother for Christmas."

"I hate it when you're right," she mumbled, but curled up against his shoulder again, where it was warm and inviting.

CHAPTER NINE

JEREMY WATCHED THE end credits roll and leaned his head back against the sofa. He could shut off the TV right now but he didn't want to disturb Tori, who had finally drifted off just before the courtroom verdict in the movie. She'd missed the happy ending, the perfect house and family and a new brother on the way. Emotion clogged his throat for a moment as he turned his head an inch and looked down at her, lashes against her cheeks, warm belly pressed against his hip.

She would be so easy to love, if he were capable of it.

As it was, he definitely had feelings for her. She was the purest person he'd ever known. Always seemed to find a bright side, a positive angle. Cared about people.

Cared about him.

At least she made him believe she did. And she was snuggled up to him right now, trusting.

He felt pretty damned unworthy of that.

The credits ended and the app went to a home

screen with "suggested for you" thumbnails of other holiday movies. It wasn't late, but it was late enough, and clearly she was exhausted. She'd been working long hours for days, and carrying the baby, too.

As carefully as he could, he shifted his hips so that her head was cradled in his elbow, then turned so that he was off the sofa, leaning over her. With as much gentleness as he could muster, he slipped an arm beneath her legs and the other beneath her shoulders, keeping her head snug against him. He lifted her in his arms and adjusted her weight as her lashes fluttered.

"Jeremy?"

"Shh… You fell asleep. I'm taking you to bed."

He got halfway down the hall before she actually lifted her head. "You really are carrying me. You're going to give yourself a hernia."

He couldn't stop the burst of laughter that started in his chest. Lord, but she made him laugh sometimes at the most unexpected moments.

"I'm pretty sure I can handle it," he replied.

He nudged open the door to her room and laid her down on the bed, but she was awake now and scooted up so that she was sitting. "That was very sweet of you."

"I was hoping I wouldn't wake you. You looked so peaceful."

"I was comfortable." She smiled, the edges of it soft from sleep. "You're kind of warm and cozy."

Jeremy went to the bed and sat on the edge. "Honestly? I don't think I've ever been called that before."

"Well, you are. And I need to be awake anyway, because I need to pee and brush my teeth." She put her hand on his forearm. "It was a really nice night. A nice day, when all is said and done. Thank you."

He reached over to pat her hand and ended up taking her fingers in his instead, twining them together, linking them in a way that frightened him just a bit. Still, this was what he'd suggested, wasn't it? Acknowledgment of their attraction for each other? Desire? Affection? His thumb rubbed over the top of her hand, and he met her gaze, saying nothing. The air between them grew heavy with words unspoken, possibilities unrealized.

"You're going to kiss me, aren't you?" she murmured, but instead of looking away, as she had a tendency to do, she held his gaze.

"Only if you want me to."

She said nothing for a few seconds that felt like an eternity, and he waited, trying to be patient. Wanting to leave this decision in her hands.

"You want me to say it." She bit down on her lip, another thing he realized she did when she was nervous.

"Yeah," he replied, his voice rough. "I do."

Another long moment, and then she said it, her voice barely above a whisper. "Kiss me, Jeremy. Please."

She didn't have to ask twice, or even add the sweet-sounding "please" to the end. "Kiss me" was enough. He squeezed her fingers tighter and leaned forward. "No mistletoe in here," he murmured, only an inch away from her lips.

"We don't need it," she answered, and he closed the remaining distance between them.

Nothing in the world could be as soft as her lips. They opened beneath his, sweet and willing, and an expansive feeling rushed through him as he drank her in. He inched closer, close enough that if he moved his arm at all it would be around her and pulling her close, but tonight she was in charge. She set the pace. He'd kissed her twice already. Tonight he wanted—needed—to know that she wanted him as much as he wanted her.

As the kiss deepened, she leaned forward, moving to get closer to him, and before they lost their balance he put out his left hand and braced it on the bed. Tori curled her hand up around his neck and exerted a little pressure, pulling him closer to her, then shifting so that she was slowly inching downward with him leaning over her from above. Desire surged; last summer hadn't been a fluke, and she still had the power to make him weak and strong at the same time. Their chemistry couldn't be ignored as she made a little sound in the back of her throat. He slid his mouth off hers and pressed his lips to the sensitive spot on her neck where her pulse drummed.

"Oh," she breathed, arching her neck. "Jeremy... That feels so nice."

"Damn right," he growled, fighting to keep his hands gentle.

"Jeremy, I—" Another sigh stopped her mid-sentence, but she picked up again, undaunted. "Can we just kiss tonight?"

She had to know what she was asking. He wanted to touch her everywhere. Feel her warm, smooth skin against his. But he'd promised himself that she could take the lead and so he dutifully answered, "Of course."

"You're a good kisser."

"Mmm... Likewise."

"You've got SKL. Do you know what that is?"

"Uh-uh." He licked at her earlobe and goose bumps erupted on her shoulders as he slid his fingers along the skin revealed by the slouchy sweater's neckline. It had a V-neck, and with it pulled a bit sideways, a generous slice of cleavage and the swell of her full breast were visible before the rest was concealed by her bra.

"Seriously kissable lips. Not too full, not too

thin, really nice and soft. With that little dip in the middle, right here." She slid her hand from his hair down his jaw, then dotted the dip in his upper lip with a fingertip.

"Tori?"

"Yeah?"

"You talk too much."

And then he went to work shutting her up. Because if she wanted to be kissed—and that was all she wanted—he'd give her what she asked for. And he'd do it right.

Tori rolled over in bed the next morning and stared at the ceiling. The events of last night were crammed in her brain, one on top of the other, until everything was clouded with Jeremy.

She'd intended to be cautious. Said she only wanted kissing. But she'd been mistaken if she'd thought kissing him gave her any sort of protection. Instead, Jeremy Fisher and his clever mouth had sneaked past all her defenses.

It was a good thing that he had no idea how close she'd been to inviting him to stay in her bed. Just when she'd reached the point where she was ready to ask for more, he'd pulled back, kissed the tip of her nose, and wished her good-night.

She supposed she had to add honorable to his list of qualities, too. Instead of being comforted, the thought set her on edge. It couldn't be this simple. There was something about him that had to be flawed, something that was going to go wrong. She wished she had some idea what it was so she could prepare herself for it. She definitely didn't want to be blindsided again.

She got up and went to the bathroom for a refreshing shower, then dressed in tights and a swing-type dress from her "before pregnant" wardrobe that accommodated her growing tummy nicely, at least at this stage. The neckline looked a bit bare, so she found an infinity scarf and wound it around her neck, then put her hair up in a messy bun. She looked in the mirror with a critical eye. Back home this would be dressing up. But here... It was a different atmosphere. Different expectations, too.

Jeremy was in the kitchen, pouring cereal into a bowl. "Good morning. There's decaf if you want it."

Her outfit would be completed with her black boots, but inside she was in her stockinged feet and felt a little vulnerable. She tried a smile, wondering how he could act so normal while inside she was still stuck on last night's kisses and him carrying her to the bedroom.

"I'd like that."

"I'll get it. Help yourself to what you want for breakfast. There's bread for toast, or cereal, and fresh eggs. Or smoothies. I keep stuff on hand for shakes. It's what I normally eat, though today I felt like cereal."

He was quite the conversationalist in the morning, she thought, accepting the mug of coffee he handed over, fixed the way she liked—how had he remembered that?

"You look nice today," he added, touching her arm on his way past her with his cereal bowl. Instead of eating at the dining room table, he perched on a bar stool at a high counter. It was far more comfortable than the huge table and formal setting.

She stuck her head in the refrigerator so he wouldn't see her blush. "Thanks. And there are berries! Excellent."

She turned around and saw Jeremy's eyes flit up to her face. He'd been staring at her backside as she looked in the fridge.

"Sorry," he said, without sounding too sorry at all. "I got distracted by your butt."

Her lips twitched. "You really don't beat around the bush, do you?"

"I try not to."

"Well, then, stop looking at my butt and tell me what's on the agenda today."

She sat next to him on a high stool and arranged berries and melon on a plate. Took a sip of coffee and put the mug down, tried to pretend this was as normal as could be.

"Well, I thought you might like to do some shopping."

"You don't have to buy me things, you know. I have clothes."

"Sure, but how often do you get to shop on Fifth Avenue? Come on, surely there are stores you'd like to go into. Besides, you actually need a few things. Like a coat. Your regular winter one is getting snug already. You're not going to make it through to March or April and still be able to zip it up."

He was right about the coat; she'd already realized it. "Well, I can get one back home."

"And you can get one here. Let me spoil you a little. Besides, I need a new tie."

"Sure you do."

He wiggled his eyebrows. "So, I probably don't. But I can't in all conscience bring you here for a week and not take you shopping. We can walk. And this afternoon I have a surprise for you."

She paused, a piece of honeydew on her fork. "What kind of a surprise?"

"Nope. Not going to get it out of me that easily."

"I don't know, Jeremy. This makes me uncomfortable. I can't ever possibly pay you back."

He frowned. "Why would I want you to do that? Look, Tori. I have more money than I know what to do with, frankly, and rarely have anyone to spend it on. This is a treat for me to do this for you, okay? A gift, nothing more."

"Well, I can't reciprocate, either."

"I don't need you to. Buying you a few clothes, taking you to see a few new things… If I promise not to shower you with jewels, are we okay?"

What could she say? He was right. A day's shopping was a drop in the bucket to him, so why should it bother her so much?

Because it made her feel as if she owed him something.

And she couldn't say that to him without insulting him. Especially when he'd been so very nice to her already. Never pushing. Not once had he given her any indication he had a hidden agenda or was trying to manipulate her or the situation. She was the one coming up with that scenario, purely out of fear.

Maybe it was as her mom said. Sometimes you had to have a little faith.

By the time early afternoon arrived, Tori was laden with bags, most of which contained what she'd been wearing that morning. Her boots were in a boot box and new ones cradled her feet and calves; she wore the same swing dress and tights of the morning but the scarf was replaced with a new checked one of wool and silk. Instead of her everyday jacket, which was now tucked in another box in a huge bag, she wore a cashmere cape and gloves that Jeremy had insisted he buy her. Add in the sunglasses and she was pretty sure today's ensemble came to more than she'd spent on the down payment for her house.

She felt both glamorous and a fraud, beautiful and a bit not-quite-herself, but today's shopping had been an experience. Brands she'd only ever seen online or in magazines were now on her body.

Jeremy had also insisted she buy some maternity clothes, so he'd taken her into Saks, where he'd slapped down his credit card for two pairs of pants, three tops and two dresses—one that she could wear for any occasion, and the other a cocktail dress. When she protested that one, he'd insisted that sometime over Christmas she might like to dress up. She'd countered by saying she'd be overdressed in something so expensive, and then he'd raised an eyebrow at her and she'd given up. Maybe she would have fought harder if she didn't absolutely love the navy dress, but from the moment she'd put it on, it had been perfect. Then it was off to buy shoes. She'd reached her limit when he came around a corner with a plump, plush penguin in his hand. "And something for the baby, too," he'd said, flashing her a smile.

He carried most of the bags while she held the ones containing the penguin and the dresses. They'd started walking back toward the park— at least that was what she thought if her sense of direction was right—when he stopped and lifted his chin at something over his shoulder.

She turned around and looked. It was the same spot they'd been the day before, just steps away from The Plaza.

"Tea?"

Her mouth dropped open. "Are you serious?"

He nodded. "I got us in for three o'clock, and since we didn't stop for lunch, you must be famished. Today you can be Eloise and have high tea at The Plaza."

"Jeremy."

He laughed at her tone of voice. "Yes?"

"I do not know how you pulled this off. Do people really live like this? I don't believe it."

His eyes shone at her. "Every day? No. Once in a while? Everyone should. Just once in their lifetime, I think."

"I'm afraid I'll get something on me. Seriously." She knew the cape had cost far too much. Right now wasn't life, it was pretending. But she couldn't help it. She'd pretend for a little while longer, because it was amazing.

"Come on. It's ten to three, and we'll get there

just in time. You can even freshen up a bit before we're seated."

When they walked in the door, her head nearly swiveled all the way around. The lobby was stunning in and of itself, but when Jeremy led her to The Palm Court, she had to catch her breath.

Light. And elegance. And green palms and the most amazing ceiling…the iconic stained glass dome. She couldn't believe she was here.

"Tori? Tori." Jeremy was at her side, touching her elbow. "It's going to be a few minutes. Come on, we can leave our bags with the concierge and pick them up when we're done. I'll show you where the powder room is."

She tore herself away from the sight and followed him, her boots clicking on the floor. In the powder room she tidied her hair and refreshed her lipstick. There were roses in her cheeks; partly from the fresh, cold air and partly because of excitement, she was sure. She found Jeremy again and he solicitously took her cape, draping it over his arm for the time being.

When they were led to their table, she looked around at all the other people having tea. Some were dressed more casually than she. Others were dressed impeccably from head to toe, without a hair out of place. At her seat, she placed a hand on her tummy as she sat, tucking the skirt of her dress beneath her.

"So. Surprised?"

"Very," she responded, unable to stop staring. "Oh, look at this place. And how did you ever get a table on such short notice? I've always heard that it takes weeks or months to get in for tea."

"I pulled some strings," he admitted. "While you were asleep yesterday."

Of course he had.

"Look at the menu," he suggested. "I'll say everything's good, but you should make your selections based on what you like. Especially if there's something the baby doesn't like, or you can't eat while you're pregnant."

She lifted her gaze to his. "Has someone been doing some reading?"

"Maybe. When I sent the grocery list to my housekeeper—Melissa, by the way—I wanted to get some things you like and…well, healthy things."

She pointed to the list of sweets on the tea menu. "These are not healthy, and I am going to enjoy several."

He laughed. "Good."

He ordered a plain black tea for himself, while Tori went for a more aromatic Earl Grey. All around them was the clink of silverware on china, the hum of conversations. Tea arrived, and their tray of delights—finger sandwiches of cucumber, salmon, and turkey, perfect scones with Devonshire cream and lemon curd, and a selection of pastries and sweets that nearly made her teeth ache just looking at them. The entire hour, eating and chatting and people watching, was a dream come true. No matter what happened in their future, she'd always have this day to remember.

She'd told him once she wasn't Cinderella, but she was surely feeling like it now. She was in the hotel business, was assistant manager to an upscale resort, but the Sandpiper and all its wonderful amenities paled in comparison to this.

It was like a mansion being compared to a palace.

"Have the last scone," Jeremy suggested. "I can tell you love the cream with the preserves."

They were a bit of heaven for sure. She didn't argue, didn't protest, just reached for the light-as-air scone and smeared it with strawberry, then topped it with cream and popped it in her mouth.

"I love watching you eat," he said, a smile lighting his face.

She nearly choked on a crumb. "Er...what?"

"I just mean you like food. You don't pretend not to."

Oh, goodness. He was probably used to stick women who starved themselves or something. Or perhaps her manners were lacking. How mortifying.

"Don't worry, it's a compliment. You're real, Tori. It's one of the things I like about you."

"Are you sure? Because I'm pretty confident I have scone crumbs on my dress now and sadly when we get home and I take these boots off my ankles are probably going to swell from all the walking and stuff we did today."

"Real," he repeated. "Flesh and blood. No pretending to be someone you're not, no putting on airs to try to impress me. You are who you are and you're comfortable with it. That kind of confidence is rare."

She didn't know what to say. She was very aware that she'd gained a few pounds with the baby and some of it was due to potato chips. And until now, she hadn't really cared. She understood he was paying her a compliment. But she hadn't considered confidence before. "I mean, I guess I just am who I am. I'm not sure I can change for anyone, or be a chameleon."

"I would hope not." He leaned forward. "Because you're normal, you see? And when I'm with you, I feel normal, too."

"Are you lonely, Jeremy?"

"Sometimes. I have my friends and all, and my sister and I are semi close, but it's not the same as being…"

This time his voice drifted off, and he looked away for a moment.

"Intimate with someone?"

His gaze came back to hers. "Yeah. And not just physically, though that's not a problem with you either, it seems."

The baby must have enjoyed the tea as well, because it was moving around fairly consistently. She absently rubbed a hand over the curve, mindlessly soothing. But Jeremy noticed, and his face softened.

"I want us to be a family somehow. You should know that."

Nerves quivered in her stomach. "We will be. No matter what we decide to do. Because we're going to raise this baby together. Okay?"

He nodded.

When their tea was cleared away, he helped her put her cape back on, tenderly buttoning the top button. She picked up her new wristlet containing her phone and cards, and as Jeremy placed his hand along the small of her back, she caught a glimpse of a woman, probably in her fifties, watching them with a soft smile on her face. Tori smiled back shyly and as they passed the woman's table, she said, "Congratulations."

"Oh! Thank you," she answered, pressing her hand on her belly as a reflex.

Right now she felt as if they *were* a family. But the day was pretend. Wasn't it?

CHAPTER TEN

THE WEEK TURNED into a whirlwind, and Jeremy tried to hit every iconic New York experience he could think of.

One evening he took her to the Christmas Spectacular with the Rockettes at Radio City Music Hall, and they watched them kick their way through a dance routine that would have had him winded in about thirty seconds. Tori's eyes had shone as she focused on the stage, her smile bright as she turned to him time and again throughout the show.

Then there were the frenetic lights and sounds of Times Square, filled with tourists. It wasn't his favorite spot, but she'd wanted to see where the ball would drop on New Year's Eve. He showed her, and vowed to himself that one day he'd bring her here on December 31 so she could see it for real.

Of course, no trip to Times Square could be enjoyed without a piece of cheesecake from Junior's, and he bought her pineapple because he thought it was the best. He hadn't been wrong, it seemed, because she'd savored every bite, laughingly proclaiming that it was for the baby.

There'd been pizza one night, sitting on the carpet and finally watching the original *Miracle on 34th Street*, and slow but sweet kisses stolen here and there. A trip up the Empire State Building, where she'd held his hand as she looked out over the city, and a more sobering visit to the 9/11 Memorial.

Alas, he couldn't avoid work altogether, and he'd been sneaking the odd hour here and there to look after things that couldn't wait. He had to go into his office, though, so he left her the keys and told her to have a relaxing day, wherever that might take her. She'd made noises about wanting to visit the park again, or maybe go to the Met. Both were practically on his doorstep, so he left with no worries about how she'd spend the day.

At one o'clock, he realized he hadn't eaten lunch, so he decided to pop down to the bottom floor and the restaurant on-site. Before he could get out of the office door, however, two familiar faces came toward him down the hall.

"The two of you here together? Something big must be up."

Cole Abbott flashed a grin. "Well, Bran said he was coming to see you, and I was going to be in the city, so I thought I'd tag along."

They exchanged backslapping hugs, then Jeremy turned back around toward his office. "It's good to see you two."

"Bran said you had some news. Wouldn't tell me what it is, though."

Cole scowled at his companion. Bran was smiling, but it didn't quite reach his eyes, and his cheeks still looked hollow from grief. Jeremy knew exactly what had brought Cole to the city. Worry for their friend.

"Bran's bought a house in Nova Scotia. Did he tell you that?"

"Yes, so I know that's not the news. What's up?"

Jeremy took a moment to look out his office window. He had a great view of the Hudson. He had just about everything a man could want.

He faced the men again and let out a breath. "Well, I'm going to be a father."

Branson stared at Cole, who sat heavily in a chair in front of Jeremy's desk. He let out a curse word and ran his hand over his face. "For real?"

Jeremy laughed. "Yeah. Needless to say, it was a surprise for me, too."

"Who is she? When? How did it happen?"

"Tori, last summer, and the usual way."

Branson laughed, the sound rusty. "Oh, man. Your face, Cole. This is why I didn't tell you."

Jeremy chuckled. "It's not the end of the world, dude."

"Are you sure?"

"We're all nearly thirty-six years old. It was bound to happen to one of us eventually."

Silence fell. Jeremy suddenly wished he could cut out his tongue. It had happened—to Bran. And then it had been ripped away. All his happiness.

"Oh, Bran, I'm sorry. That was thoughtless."

Bran waved a hand. "Forget it."

"I can't. I'm so, so—"

Bran looked him dead in the eye. "It's okay, Jeremy. Really. I can't pretend it didn't happen, and you guys can't tap-dance around it for the rest of your lives. So shut up and tell us what's happening. Because last I heard you were in Canada finding out the news and freaking out a bit."

Jeremy perched on the edge of the desk as the tension in the room dissipated a bit. "Well, she's here, actually. I brought her here for a week so we could talk about what we want to do."

"Are you guys a thing?"

"I don't know. Yes? But no. I mean, we haven't slept together."

"Clearly you did…"

"I mean since I found out." He aimed a "smart aleck" look at Cole. "But I like her, a lot. And she likes me. And we've kissed…"

Bran nudged Cole. "This is nearly as bad as when we were freshmen and he was telling us about the girl he'd left behind… What was her name? Jill? Jane? Though I think he said he'd felt her up once."

"Again, shut up. I don't know why we're still friends." But a smile curved up his cheek. This was exactly why they were friends, and had been for over twenty years.

"So what, you brought her here? Is she going to move here to be with you? So you can bring the baby up together?"

"We haven't really talked about it."

"But that's what you want, right?" Bran always got to the heart of the matter.

"Yeah." He let out a breath. "I just can't see us living in two different countries and trying to parent. I'm kind of hoping that she'll like it here enough to consider moving."

"Wow." Cole sat back in the chair. "So then what? Marriage? Are you thinking of staying in your place, or buying elsewhere? Your place isn't really one where I can picture kids running around."

Jeremy frowned. "I can always redecorate. And there's room. Plus it's close to everything."

"I don't know, man. It's a lot to ask of a woman. To pack up and leave everything behind." This from Bran.

Cole scoffed. "Yeah, leave behind what? Jeremy's loaded. She's landed herself in clover."

Jeremy pushed away from the desk. "It's not like that. She doesn't care about money. And don't roll your eyes," he said in response to Cole's facial expression. "It's true. If anyone has any ulterior motives here, it's me." He sighed. "Mom and Bruce are having a party in a few days. I'm going to take her. If we do this, she's got to have her eyes wide open." He nodded at Bran. "That was your advice, and I think you're right."

"You're springing the Wicked Witch of the West on her?"

Again, Jeremy couldn't help but laugh at Cole. "Yeah, I am. But Sarah's going, too." He was thrilled his sister had agreed. He hadn't told her about Tori either, but she'd be an ally.

"Damn, brother."

"I know."

There was quiet for a moment, and then Cole said, with a bit of wonder in his voice, "You're gonna be a dad."

"Seems like it."

He got up and clapped Jeremy on the back. "Congratulations, man. You're gonna nail this."

Nope, he wasn't going to cry over this unexpected gesture. Cole was not the touchy-feely type. So he chuckled instead. "You think? Because I had a crappy example."

"Didn't we all? So just do the exact opposite

of what your mom and stepdad did and you'll be great."

Bran stood up. "And if the city thing doesn't work out, maybe we'll be neighbors, Jeremy."

Cole looked at them both.

"His new house is less than an hour away from Tori," Jeremy confirmed. "Have you seen it?" He went to his computer and brought the pics up on the monitor. "Look at that. Lighthouse and everything."

Cole tapped his lips. "How much?"

"Just under three."

"You're joking."

"Nope. You looking for an investment property?"

"I might. I've been floating a few ideas around for something. We can talk in the new year."

"Sure."

Bran coughed. "I don't know about you ladies, but I came for lunch. Let's go get a steak somewhere."

"Okay, but I can't be late getting home. I left Tori on her own today."

Bran laughed and clapped him on the shoulder. "And so it begins, bro. And so it begins."

Jeremy took the teasing with a smile. Yeah, they were right and they were ribbing him about it. But it occurred to him that he really didn't mind at all.

* * *

Tori had spent the day walking in the park, having a sandwich in a small shop somewhere and then window-shopping. She'd found this little store in Midtown that had an appealing array of housewares in the window, and inside was even better. Now, as she waited for Jeremy to come home, she looked at the items she'd bought and fought against nerves. What if he didn't like the changes? What if he resented her stepping in and doing anything to his space?

She had receipts. She could take it all back.

The kitchen smelled good, too. She'd stopped at a market and bought the groceries required to make her curried chicken and broccoli casserole. She'd made a salad, too.

The casserole was almost ready and she was watching another holiday movie on TV when Jeremy came through the door. "Wow, something smells great in here," he said from the foyer.

Score one. She got up from the sofa and went to the foyer to greet him as he hung up his coat.

"Hi. I made dinner. Not that Melissa isn't a great cook, but I like to cook and since I was at loose ends today…"

"No explanation required. I'm glad you got out today."

"I did! I had fun."

He stepped into the main living area and stopped short. "What the—? You decorated."

"Only a little." She folded her hands in front of her. "You didn't have anything up for Christmas, and it felt a little…monochrome in here."

He unbuttoned his suit jacket and loosened his tie, staying quiet long enough that her nerves bubbled up again. "I think that was the decorator's objective," he said. "To let the space speak for itself."

"Oh." His lukewarm response let all the air out of her joy balloon. She'd wanted it to be a lovely surprise. To see his face light up. Now she was just let down.

He pulled off his tie and stuffed it into his pants pocket while she stood there, unsure of what to do next. She rather liked the little three-foot tree she'd bought, decorated with white lights and red and silver bows. The poinsettia centerpiece she'd had delivered from the florist graced the center of the dining table. The air smelled of pine boughs and cones from the candle arrangement on the glass coffee table. A small gift bag sat on the table, too, and her eyes stung. He didn't like it.

She wouldn't be so obvious as to move his present right away. She'd wait until he moved somewhere else and sneak it away to her room, or perhaps in the drawer of the table. She could return it tomorrow. Return everything.

"I have receipts," she whispered.

"What?"

"Receipts. To take everything back. I know it was presumptuous of me. This is your home. I just thought…it could use some Christmas spirit in here."

He looked at her strangely, then turned his back and went to the kitchen. She rushed over to the table, grabbed the gift bag and tucked it into the drawer where he kept his remotes and magazines.

"There's a rooster in my kitchen!"

Tori froze. Oh, God, was he angry? She pressed her hand to her chest and pursed her lips, letting out a slow breath. Up until now, he'd been so easygoing. It was one of the things she liked about him. But his living space… It didn't fit with the Jeremy she had spent time with so far. It was colorless and without humor. Without life. She puckered her eyebrows. That made no sense. How could decor have a sense of humor? But it was how she felt just the same. He was larger than life. His apartment was…prescriptive.

She went into the kitchen and prepared herself for, at the very least, an annoyed Jeremy.

He was staring at the ceramic rooster she'd bought, sitting in the middle of the counter. She suddenly felt a wave of irritation sweep over her. All she'd done was add a few holiday decorations and buy a stupid knickknack. He didn't have to be so…cold. It wasn't like him, or at least the Jeremy she knew.

Maybe the problem was she didn't know him at all.

"Your place is boring, Jeremy. You needed a conversation piece, and I got you one." She put her hands on her hips.

His head swiveled and he stared at her for a long moment, and then the most surprising thing happened. He started laughing. A low chuckle, almost despite himself, and her lips twitched. Then harder, and she tried really hard not to laugh back. But when he let loose and bent over, laughing himself silly, she couldn't help it. She started laughing, too, until they were both breathless.

"A…a…conversation piece," he choked out, still laughing. "A rooster. Oh, my God."

Oh, goodness. He was too adorable right now. And not mad. She didn't know what he was feeling, not really, but he wasn't mad at her, and her relief was great.

The oven timer dinged and she took a deep breath. "I have to stop laughing so I can take that out of the oven."

"What is it?"

She looked at the rooster, looked at Jeremy and said, deadpan, "Chicken."

That set them off again.

It wasn't that funny. Maybe the stress of the last few weeks was getting to them.

She got the casserole out of the oven and put it on the stove to cool. Jeremy had finally stopped laughing and leaned over her shoulder to look at the dish. "Hmm. Not familiar. But it smells good."

"It is good. You wait and see." She slid off the oven mitts and turned around. He was close to her, so close her heart started a pitter-patter that she both loved and hated. "Do you really hate the decorations?" She wanted the truth now that the awkwardness had passed.

He shook his head, his gaze sobering. "No, I don't. I just wasn't prepared."

"For what? Christmas?"

"For it to look like home."

The pitter-patter turned to solid thumping. "Why? Why shouldn't your home look like a home?"

"I don't know. And this... Look, Tori. I'm just overwhelmed. I came home to you today. To an apartment with holiday decorations and a woman pregnant with my child and a home-cooked meal. I have no idea what to do with that."

How cold had his life been?

"You must have had Christmas trees."

"Not like this. Not...for me. You did this for me, didn't you?"

She nodded slightly.

Ignoring the hot casserole dish behind her, he put his hands on the edge of the cold stove and leaned in to kiss her. Really kiss her, with not only skill but with enough emotion that she turned to mush. Could they make this work? He hadn't responded because he was overwhelmed. Because he'd been floored by the idea that someone had done that for him... Her heart broke a little for the lonely boy he must have been. And now he was kissing her as if she'd given him the moon. She'd spent no more than he'd spent on tea yesterday, but she felt as if she'd given him the world.

It would be so easy to fall in love with this Jeremy. Not just the man who'd been a fantastic lover in the summer sun, or the guy who'd treated her like a princess yesterday, but this man, who let her glimpse his heart. Who could be absolutely tender with her when she needed it most.

His body fit so perfectly against hers, even with the baby between them. Over the last week she'd seen a difference in her bump, and the recent snug waistlines had given way to full-on showing. With Jeremy kissing her like she was something precious, and his baby growing within her, she felt both incredibly feminine and extraordinarily powerful in such a beautiful, natural way.

He'd given that to her. And it was worth more than some artificial tree with a few lights and bows.

And when he broke the kiss and hugged her, she felt herself slipping further under his spell.

"Thank you. I'm sorry I didn't say it before. I love that you thought of me and wanted to do this for me. I don't think I've ever really had that before."

"Then I'm glad I did it because everyone deserves to feel seen and important," she answered, holding on to his shoulders. She slid her fingers into his hair. "You're a lot of things, Jeremy, but you're also a man, and you're human."

He kissed her again, long and slow, and she gave herself over to the emotion of the moment. He'd asked her here so they could see where they were in their relationship. What if this could work somehow? What if there really was a happy ending? She tried not to worry about logistics. Those weren't really what concerned her at this point. It was Jeremy, and whether they could parent together, if they could be together. A couple *and* a family.

Right now, all the signs pointed to yes, because he was threading his hands through her hair and she was reaching for the buttons on his shirt.

She was halfway down his chest when he put his hand over hers. "You sure?" he asked, a little hint of sexy gravel in his voice. "You have to be sure."

"I'm sure." She lifted her chin. "I want you. All of you."

Including his heart. And maybe that wouldn't happen today. But she hoped it would someday, because his was a heart worth cherishing.

CHAPTER ELEVEN

JEREMY HAD NEVER once been scared before making love to a woman, but he was scared tonight.

There was a lot at stake. A ton of possibility that could be the best thing ever to happen to him—or he could blow it and they'd be back to square one, just like they were in her office the day he'd discovered she was pregnant.

But more than that, he'd never before made love to a woman where his heart was involved, and it was with Tori. As much as he tried to deny it, she touched something inside him he usually kept locked away. And he'd let her get a glimpse of it. He didn't like being that vulnerable.

She was standing in his room now, facing him, the soft light of a pair of lamps illuminating her pale skin. He moved forward, wanting to undress her, as scared as he'd been his very first time. Her gaze locked with his, her eyes warmed and her lips curved up in a small smile.

"Don't be scared," she said, as if she could read his thoughts.

"I want to see you." His heart clubbed against his ribs as he reached for her sweater, bunching it up in his hands until it went past her waist, over her breasts, over her head. When her hair was free she shook it out, and he dropped the sweater. Her full breasts were cupped by a plain black satin bra, and her leggings came up over her bump. Holding his gaze, she pushed the waistband down until she was standing before him in the bra and matching underwear, the bikini elastic sitting low below where her tummy began to curve.

She was so beautiful. He could stare at her forever, marveling at how gorgeous she was and the awesomeness of her carrying their child.

"Are you going to touch me?" she asked, tilting her head.

He reached out and put his hand on her hip, pulling her closer, and lifted his other hand to her ribs, skimming over her thickened waist, his thumb roving toward her breast. Dammit, his hands were shaking.

She put her fingers on his face, guiding him to look her in the eyes. "I need to know, Jeremy. Need to know that this is still good and real. We have a lot to figure out, but most of all we need to decide how we feel about each other."

"You think I have a choice? That I can decide?" He was already a goner.

"Maybe *decide* is the wrong word. Maybe *acknowledge*." Her fingers traced over his jaw, the fingernail scraping his stubble a little bit. "Me, here with you, like this… I'm acknowledging that I feel something for you."

"I don't take this lightly," he murmured.

"Nor do I. So when you touch me…when you take me…know that I've made this choice tonight. Knowing the risks and wanting you anyway."

He was afraid. Humbled. He almost considered not going through with it, and then she moved toward him, pressing her lips to the hollow between his shoulder and collarbone. He shuddered and closed his eyes, drinking in the sensation, the tenderness, the heat of it. Their time together in the summer had been nothing short of spectacular. With the news of the baby and walking on eggshells, he'd nearly forgotten. But not now. Not with her so close to him with his shirt spread open and their skin touching, warm and soft.

He let out a shaky sigh, then gathered her against him and shut out the world.

Tori rolled over and felt the sheets gathered beneath her armpits. They were silk, black silk, and caressed her body as she shifted to face Jeremy.

He was still sleeping on his back, his lips relaxed and his lashes resting peacefully.

She was wearing nothing but her bikini panties again, which she vaguely remembered pulling on before sliding back into bed and into his arms, falling into sleep.

That had been two hours ago, around eight o'clock. Right now, her belly rumbled and the baby kicked all at the same time. They hadn't eaten dinner.

"Someone's hungry."

Her breath caught at the sound of his amused voice. His eyes were still closed, but the corners of his mouth twitched.

"I am. And so's your kid. Besides, that casserole is cold now and we should eat it and then put the leftovers in the fridge."

"But you're warm and snuggly."

Snuggly wasn't the word she'd use. Her breasts were heavier now and more sensitive with the pregnancy, and the slippery sheets felt almost like a caress. She was nearly naked in bed with him; that was distraction enough. But she was also starving. And truthfully, she was still reeling from what had happened between them. She needed some distance to make sense of her thoughts.

It had been good between them before. Tonight had been…better. Because it wasn't just a fling anymore. Their connection had been transcendent.

She shook her head and figured that kind of thinking was going to get her into trouble. They still had to figure out this parenting thing with clear heads. Regretfully, she slipped out of the sheets and went searching for her bra.

"Here." He got out of bed and, fully naked, went to the closet and took out a soft robe. "Put this on if you don't want to get all dressed up again."

It was charcoal gray and thick and soft, and she wrapped it around her body while his scent rose from the fabric. "Thanks," she murmured.

And tried not to look at his butt when he went back to the closet, but she failed. It was a rather spectacular backside.

He returned wearing a pair of plaid sleep pants and a sweatshirt. It shouldn't have been attractive, but it made her want to crawl inside his embrace again.

They went to the kitchen and Tori scooped up servings of casserole and put them in the microwave. While they were heating, she put the rest in containers and put them in the fridge, next to the salad that had never been touched. Jeremy filled water glasses, and within moments they were seated at the counter again, chowing down on the chicken, broccoli and rice with creamy sauce.

"This is delicious."

"It's my mom's recipe. I don't know where she got it, but she used to make it now and again, especially for potlucks."

He took a sip of water. "Potlucks?"

She laughed. "Okay, so not everyone in the world caters their functions. A potluck is where you have a gathering of some kind and everyone brings a dish. It's awesome because you get this amazing variety of food. Some people just stop at the grocery store and get platters of veggies and stuff, you know? But then other people bring amazing dishes. We had a neighbor who always made meatballs. A guy from church who came with a ton of hot chicken wings. And don't get me started on the salads and cheeses and appetizers…"

He laughed, scooping up more food. "It sounds fun."

"It is. And if it's a kitchen party, then you also bring your own alcohol and someone is likely to bring a guitar and it gets fun and rowdy."

His face took on a faraway expression. "What?" she asked.

"I don't think I've ever had that in my life."

She patted his hand. "Where I come from, few people are rolling in cash. Everyone chips in, good times had by all. It's what happens in a community."

"In my community, people decorate and cater and send out invitations and try to impress each other."

"Sounds dreadful."

Now his face was downright pensive. "I'm sorry to hear that, because my mom is holding something quite similar to that on Saturday, at our house in Connecticut. I want you to come."

All the warmth that had been flooding through her body froze. "Oh, no. Meet the parents? Not likely."

He pushed his plate aside, and she did, too. She didn't have much appetite left.

"Tori, after tonight, I think we need to start talking about what we plan to do. I mean, really talk about it. This whole week has been amazing and fun. But the point was also to be alone together, to decide what we want to do about us and the baby. We haven't even talked about that at all."

She nodded, looking down at the smears of sauce on her plate. "I know. I've been avoiding it because everything is going to change."

He put his hand over hers. "Would you consider moving here?"

Panic slid down her body. She was still vulnerable from the hours spent in his arms, and her hopes warred with caution. "I don't know. I don't want to say no right off the bat, but while I've enjoyed my week here, I'm not sure I'm the kind of person who can live in the middle of a huge city. Let alone Manhattan."

"We could keep this place and stay here when we want to come into the city. And I'd be willing to look at properties elsewhere that you might like better."

"Like Connecticut?"

He laughed a little. "And be that close to my family? Hell, no. Maybe more like Long Island. There are some particularly good places for young families there." He squeezed her hand. "This is my job, you know. I can find us a place, if you'll consider moving."

Was she really considering it? The idea took her breath away. "You're assuming that I'm okay with picking up and leaving my life. But I like my life. And I like working. I know I wouldn't have to provide an income for us to live off. But the Sandpiper has been my home away from home for years now. I've helped build it into the hotel it is today. It's asking a lot, to leave the life I've built behind."

"I know." He let out a sigh. "But you can work anywhere, right? Especially if it's not about the money. You could find something that you really like."

She thought about it. A big house, their baby, a job she could work at to give her purpose… never any worries about bills. She wasn't sure she trusted a future that seemed so perfect. "After what you said about your mom, I thought you'd want me to be home to look after the baby all the time."

He snorted. "My mom was home all the time and never spent a second with us. Being a good parent isn't decided on who gets to stay home and who works. Even I know that."

She smiled. "Okay, fair enough." She looked over at him. "And you're sure you don't want to come to Nova Scotia?"

"Don't get me wrong. I love the province. It's beautiful. But the market is so much smaller. I'd be bored out of my mind. And that has nothing to do with you, and everything to do with me not wanting to fall into the trap of the 'idle rich.' I need a purpose, too."

She got that. She truly did.

"There's immigration stuff to worry about. I'm not a US citizen." Especially if a marriage wasn't in the picture.

"We can get a lawyer for that."

"I suppose." She slid her hand out from beneath his. "And problems do go away easier when you can throw money at them."

It was quiet for a few moments, before Jeremy

spoke up again, his eyes telegraphing his disappointment. "That's the first time you've thrown money in my face. Are you upset?"

She felt badly, even though what she'd said was true. Solutions to problems came easier when there was lots of money to look after them. Truthfully, though, she was scared. Not angry. Just overwhelmed.

This gorgeous man, sitting in his robe, eating leftovers after making love… She was petrified of making a wrong decision. Because right now the truth was she could envision their life together and it seemed so perfect. She was pretty sure she was falling in love with him, and after what had happened earlier tonight, she thought it might be a possibility that he'd fall for her, too. He'd confided in her. And then they'd been intimate. There had been a moment when their eyes had met and it had felt as if everything clicked into place.

She just had to be brave enough.

"There's a lot of personal risk for me," she said quietly, and swiveled on her stool so she was facing him. Their knees barely touched. "Yes, it would mean both of us being there to parent our child. And yes, this week has been really promising with regards to…us. It's still a leap and a half to think about quitting my job, leaving my country and moving in with you with no guar-

antees." She patted his knee. "Please don't think I'm looking for guarantees. I'm not. It's much too soon for that."

"We can lay out any terms you want," he replied. His gaze held hers. "You can go home whenever. You know that, right? It's not just about business for me, either, Tori. The opportunities here for him or her... They're huge. I want our kid to have the best of both worlds—the opportunities I had with the love and support I didn't. But I think you did."

Would living here be so bad? Especially if there was money—which there would be—for her mom to fly here, or for her to fly home? It was a fairly short direct flight, after all. And it wasn't as if she hated his apartment; she had loved her week here and all the things New York offered. "You'd really look at moving outside the city and commuting in?"

He shrugged. "Lots of people do it. Besides, I'm not always in the city anyway. We could get a place near the water. Have a boat. Hell, we could travel up the coast to visit your mom if you wanted."

Because money was no object. Except it was all his money, and she knew she shouldn't feel guilty but did anyway.

"I'd want some sort of agreement drawn up," she said firmly. "Something stating that if this

doesn't work out, I can't go after your money. I'm not a gold digger, Jeremy."

His lips dropped open. "I know that."

"I want it in writing just the same."

"Whatever makes you happy." He slid forward on his bar stool a bit. "Tori, I know I'm asking a lot of you. In return I promise to do whatever I can to make sure you're happy and content. If that means you look for a job, so be it. If you want to stay home with the baby, that's fine, too." He put his hand on her belly. "I like you a lot, and I think you like me." That flirty smile was back on his lips. "At least the last few hours give me that impression. I have to do better than my own father did with me, you know? And if that means giving our relationship a try, then what do we have to lose? If it doesn't work, we figure out a new arrangement. But there's so much to gain, sweetheart. So much."

Damn. He'd hit her right in her vulnerable spots. She knew how much his father's abandonment had affected him. And he'd called her *sweetheart*—to her mind, the first endearment to leave his lips.

It wasn't the normal progression for a relationship, but what did that matter? He'd been wonderful from the start. Yes, they had their differences—financially, geographically—but

did that mean they couldn't have a future together? Of course not.

"Well, I'm willing to look at some options. No
guarantees, but I'm not saying no."

A brilliant smile broke over his lips. "It's a
maybe, which is way better than *no*. I'll take it.
And I can show you some examples of nice properties for us."

She also wanted to ask him about citizenship
for the baby, because she couldn't imagine having
her baby outside Canada. But that didn't have to
be decided tonight. The fact that they'd come up
with the beginnings of a plan was huge.

That she'd be facing a lot of changes meant she
had a lot to think over. Work, for example, and
how long she'd stay at the hotel before the baby
was born. Living arrangements. Possibly listing
her own house, if she decided to move.

He got up and took their plates into the kitchen,
stopping to load them in the dishwasher. "Come
on," he said, once they were out of sight. "Come
to bed and get some sleep. We have Mom's on
Saturday, but tomorrow I have another surprise
for you. Something I haven't done since I was a
kid."

"Oh?" Her interest piqued, she lifted her head
and peered around the corner at him. "What's
that?"

He came back and held out his hand. She took

it. "If I told you, it wouldn't be a surprise." He tugged on her hand, and she slipped off the stool. "But I promise you'll like it."

"You haven't steered me wrong yet," she admitted, and let herself be pulled closer, so that his arm was around her as they made their way back down the hall.

At the junction to their bedrooms, he stopped and looked into her eyes. "If you want to sleep in your own bed, I understand, but if you want to stay with me, I'd like that, too. It's your choice."

Spending the night seemed like a big deal, but then, if they were really going to give this a shot, she couldn't keep shying away from intimacy. At some point she had to trust that he was as good as he seemed.

"Your room is fine," she said, butterflies settling in her stomach at this new step in their relationship. "But I'd like to get my pajamas first, if that's okay."

"If it makes you more comfortable," he answered, tapping a fingertip on her nose and smiling. "Don't do it on my account."

Heat crept up her cheeks, but she tried to enjoy it. Sharing a child made the stakes high, but there was no reason why this couldn't turn out to be a good, healthy relationship. Why it couldn't be a real future. It was a dizzying and sobering thought.

She scurried away to get her comfy boxer shorts and top. Tonight they were sharing his room. Tomorrow, some sort of surprise. And then night after that, she was meeting his family.

If that didn't sound like a guy who was serious about moving forward, she wasn't sure what did.

CHAPTER TWELVE

JEREMY KNELT BEFORE Tori and tightened up the laces on her skate. "Is this too tight?"

"No, it feels just right."

He gave the ends another tug, then tied the knot and bow. "Okay, then. Give me your other foot."

Skating at Rockefeller Center was something he'd done as a kid. While his mom had come to the city to shop, their nanny at the time would take them skating and then off to some other adventure—and lunch—since dragging three kids around had cramped his mom's style, and his brother and sister weren't old enough to be left to their own devices. There had always been a trip to see Santa Claus, too. He'd loved that at first; his siblings had been much older and had rolled their eyes. Some years he couldn't remember; he'd been too young. Another, though, he'd asked for some video game system while sitting on Santa's lap.

Christmas morning arrived. No gaming console. His mother had been quite put out at him when he'd complained, and said how was she to know he wanted it? Maybe because he'd mentioned it only a million times and put it in his letter to Santa.

Despite that unfortunate memory, today actually brought back a lot of good ones, including lacing up skates and the hot chocolate that was to follow. Besides, as a kid, the last thing he would have wanted was to be dragged from store to store.

"Jeremy? You okay?"

He lifted his head and met her gaze. "Yeah, sorry. Just got caught up in a memory and forgot to keep tying."

"I hope it was a good one."

He smiled and tugged on the laces. "It was. I came here a lot as a kid." He gave the bow a final jerk and sat back. "There you go. All set."

She waited as he put on his own skates. "I did not expect this for a surprise today."

"It's not Christmas without the tree here and skating. And hot chocolate."

Tori pulled on thick mittens. Today she wore the older jacket that zipped up in front, which was better for skating. But she wore a new hat, he realized, and grinned. It had a hole in the top, and her dark ponytail came out and trailed down the back of her head to her neck.

Adorable was the best word to describe her right now.

"You all set?"

She nodded and held out a hand. "Let's do it."

The ice was smooth and the air crisp as they took their first gliding steps. "Be careful," he warned. "I don't want you falling down."

She laughed. "I've been skating since I was three years old. Don't worry about me." Then she twisted a little and pretended to look at her bottom. "And besides, I have lots of cushioning at the moment."

She didn't. She had curves and perhaps her figure had softened since last summer, but he found it even more alluring. Last night he'd marveled at the feel of her against him, around him. The softness of her skin and her sighs. He was in serious danger here. Thank goodness she was considering moving, because he wasn't sure what he would have said if she'd flat out refused. It wasn't just the baby, now. He wanted her with him.

She was right. The apartment was monochrome. His life was monochrome. Until she'd arrived and brought all the color and life with her.

He gave her hand a small tug, and she did a little flip so that she was skating backward and now facing him. But he held on firmly, slowing them until they were stopped. And then he slid the few inches needed to have her puffy jacket pressed against his.

"Jeremy?"

He kissed her then, on her cold, soft lips, absorbing the taste of her, the scent of her skin, the gentle pressure of her belly against him. He wasn't into showy PDA, so he let her go after a few seconds, but her eyes glittered and her cheeks were rosy.

"What was that for?"

"For being you. For agreeing to come here. For putting decorations in my apartment. For everything."

Goodness, he was feeling all sentimental and mushy, but he wouldn't always be able to hide his feelings, would he? He was sure she wasn't in love with him. She hadn't exactly leaped at the idea of moving here to be with him. But she cared, and he knew she would do whatever she thought was best for their baby. And that made her damn near perfect in his eyes.

"You're welcome. Not that I did anything."

"You've done more than you know, sweetheart."

"Come on. Let's skate. We're just standing here like idiots."

He laughed and took her hand again, and they skated around the rink, enjoying the winter air and the holiday energy and the benefit of physical exertion. They took a break for a bit and Tori took pictures of the giant Christmas tree and the statue of Prometheus.

"It's amazing at night, all lit up," he said, one arm around her waist as she leaned back against him. "But on a Friday night? Busy." He gave her a small squeeze. "Maybe next year we can come back, at night. And bring the baby, too."

The moment he said it something huge opened up inside him. Next year at this time, they would have a seven-month-old baby. They'd be a *family*. He thought about what Tori would look like, their child in her arms, breath cloudy in the frosty air, and his heart turned over. This was the right thing. He was sure of it.

"Oh, Jeremy." She sighed and leaned against him. "Are we gonna be okay? Can we really do this?"

He turned her around and looked her square in the eye. "Of course we can, and we will. Because we both know what's really important."

Her eyes shone, and she gave a sniff. "I'm falling for you, Jeremy. And scared to death because of it. I don't want to screw up the future for our baby and I don't want to set myself up for heartbreak. I'm terrified."

He didn't want to examine his own feelings too closely. Love wasn't something he did or really wanted. Love was what really hurt, and he wanted to be happy with Tori. But he could offer other assurances, couldn't he, without getting himself in too deep? "You can count on me, I promise," he said, and pulled her to him in a hug. "I've never done this before, you know. But I'm going to give you my best."

"That's all anyone can give," she said, her voice muffled against his jacket. "And I'll do the same. And we'll rely on each other, won't we?"

"Yes, sweetheart, we will."

She nodded against him and he closed his eyes as he rested his cheek along her thick hat. She was so honest and kind and willing to think the best of people. He never wanted to do anything to break the trust they had. He'd do anything to protect her and the baby. They were the most important thing now.

She gave a mighty sniff and pulled back. "Oh, I'm such an emotional wreck," she laughed, looking slightly embarrassed.

"No, you're not. If you didn't care so much, I wouldn't l…like you so much."

He'd almost said *love*. It had been right there, on the tip of his tongue, and he could tell by her wide eyes that she'd caught the slip. He couldn't say it, he couldn't give her false hope for something he wasn't capable of giving. What was most important was not repeating his parents' mistakes.

Which reminded him of the following night. The one thing he had left to do was take Bran's advice and take her to Connecticut. He didn't really want to; these days his interaction with his mother was only at special occasions. Still, if Tori was going to understand him, and his feelings about parenting, and if he wanted to have a future with her as well as his child, she had to know what she was becoming part of. Anything else wouldn't be fair.

"Let's skate some more," she suggested, and he shook off his thoughts and smiled at her. Her face was so alight with childish enthusiasm he couldn't resist.

"Okay, but I'm skating backward so you can skate forward and hold on to my hands."

"Overprotective much?"

"Indulge me."

She wiggled her eyebrows. "Okay. Maybe I'll indulge you later, too."

Now that she was starting to drop her guard, he was in even more emotional danger.

They started to circle the ice. Once, he nearly freaked because Tori let go of one hand, then did a half turn so they were both skating backward. It almost felt as if they were…dancing! Then with a laugh, she turned again, faced him, gave a push forward and slid under his arm.

"What the heck are you doing?"

She giggled. "Dancing with you!"

"Be careful."

"I'm always careful!"

In the end, though, it was Jeremy who caught an edge and felt himself go. He was holding her hand and forgot to let go; as he tumbled to the ice, he took her with him. He landed on his hip and he heard her breath leave her body with an *"oof."*

"Oh, God! Are you okay?"

She was sprawled on top of him, and she started to laugh. "Other than having the air knocked out of me? I'm fine."

He scowled. "Don't laugh! You scared me."

Her face grew tender as she looked down at him. "You gave me a soft place to fall," she whispered, and he was a goner.

If he had his way, he would always be her soft place to fall.

After skating, they had hot chocolate and cookies, and then they walked back to his apartment. His hip hurt a bit, but he was more worried about Tori. "I'm just tired," she insisted, but he wasn't so sure. Skating had probably been a bad idea. What if she'd fallen on her belly? What would have happened to the baby?

"Do you have any cramping? Any pain anywhere?"

They reached his building. "Stop fussing. Seriously, I just need a nap. I'm fine, and so is the baby."

He wasn't convinced, but he wasn't going to take chances. Once inside, he tucked her into his bed and called a doctor.

When the doctor arrived, he went in to wake Tori. She was lying on her side, her lips open, a little bit of drool clinging to the side of her mouth. She'd taken out her ponytail and her hair lay in a dark tangle on his pillowcase. Had she been right? Was she just tired? Still, it never hurt to make sure everything was okay.

"Tori?"

"Hmm?" She squeezed her eyes shut tight, and then opened them a little. "What time is it? How long did I sleep?"

"About an hour and a half. I called a doctor to come see you."

She rolled over to her back and frowned. "You called a doctor? And he's here?"

"She's here, and yes. I was worried. You got so quiet. You did have a fall, you know."

"Oh, Jeremy, you didn't have to do that. If I'd had any cramping or anything I would have said."

"Will you let her check you out anyway? It'll make me feel better."

She sighed. "Since she's already here, sure." She pushed herself up to sitting. "Let me put myself together first."

He handed her the elastic from the bedside table and watched as she deftly put her hair up again. Then he handed her a tissue. "You might have drooled a little."

"So attractive," she grumbled. "Okay, send her in. I still can't believe you got someone to make a house call."

What was the sense of having money if he couldn't use it to help the mother of his baby?

He waited outside while the doctor spoke to Tori; he'd made the decision to call but he did respect her privacy. He paced the hallway instead, wondering if there were dangers to the baby that Tori couldn't feel, chastising himself once again for taking her skating in the first place, not thinking of the dangers. Instead he'd been arrogant, thinking he'd keep her from falling when he'd been the one to take the tumble.

If anything was wrong, it was his fault.

Ten minutes after she went in, the doctor came out again. "Mr. Fisher, would you like to come in?"

Oh, no.

Tori was sitting up on the bed, a smile on her face. "I told you," she said triumphantly. "Nothing wrong."

The doctor gave her an amused look. "You still have to watch for anything abnormal, okay? And call if you start cramping or spotting."

"I will. Promise."

"So you're okay? The baby's okay?"

"If you don't trust me, will you trust her?" Tori nodded at the doctor, who was looking rather amused at the whole situation.

"She's had no cramping, no bleeding, heartbeat's steady, and she's felt the baby move. Everything seems fine. But it's always better to be safe than sorry." The doc smiled. "She said you broke her fall."

"We wouldn't have fallen if I hadn't tripped," he admitted. "I'm so sorry."

"Oh, heavens," Tori said. "It's not your fault. You can't keep me in Bubble Wrap for the next four months."

"Are you sure?"

She patted the bed. "Come sit here and listen."

He sat on one side of the bed while Tori scooted down. She'd taken off her sweatpants before sliding under the covers for her nap, so she just had to pull her shirt up as the doctor reached for a handheld machine.

"It's a portable Doppler," Tori explained. "So you can actually hear the heartbeat this time."

His own pulse took a jump. He'd calmed a bit when he'd been assured everything was okay, but now anticipation had his heartbeat accelerating. He still had the ultrasound picture tucked away in his wallet. And he'd seen the little heartbeat on the monitor before, but hearing it…

It took only seconds for the doctor to find the beat and turn up the volume, and a rapid thumping sound touched his ears.

"That's it?"

"That's it, Dad." The doctor turned the unit around so he could see. The number was 137 and the sound coming from it was his baby's tiny heart, beating inside its mother.

Tears stung his eyes and he blinked rapidly. He wouldn't cry at this moment. But he wanted to, his relief was so great. "That's the best sound in the world."

"Yup." After a few more seconds, the doctor removed the tiny wand and Tori used a cloth to wipe away the blob of gel.

The sound was gone, but he could still hear it in his head.

"Now, I've told Tori to take it easy for a day or so, just as a precaution, and the fact that it'll make you happy."

She was right it would. "Forget about my mom's tomorrow. We don't have to go."

Tori sighed. "I'm perfectly capable of going to a stuffy cocktail party for a few hours. And to be honest, I'd rather get this over with."

He couldn't blame her.

"Don't back out using me as an excuse, Jeremy."

"Fine."

The doctor merely chuckled in the background as she packed up her things.

"I'll walk you to the door," Jeremy said, erasing the scowl from his face. Besides, Tori was right.

It would be good to get it over with.

CHAPTER THIRTEEN

TORI DIDN'T KNOW why she hadn't thought to ask if Jeremy had a car. Of course he did. And the next night they left the city and headed to Connecticut, to his family home and the party that would be waiting for them.

She was dressed in the cocktail dress he'd bought her that first day of shopping, and new shoes, and the cape. She carried a little clutch and felt more than ever like Cinderella going to the ball, only this time it felt as if the host wasn't a prince but the evil stepmother.

By the time they left it was dark, so Tori couldn't even focus on the scenery. Instead, nerves bubbled up inside her. Jeremy had said that she had to know what she was getting herself into, and that didn't bode well. She had enough anxiety for the both of them; she didn't need to be absorbing any of Jeremy's. His hands gripped the steering wheel and his jaw was set. He wasn't looking forward to this holiday party, either.

"Just remember that it doesn't matter what my mother thinks of you, okay? Or Bruce, either."

"So why is it so important for me to meet them? I mean, I don't want to say that I think being estranged is a good thing, but I'm just..." She took a breath and let out what she was really thinking. "Are you hoping that it'll scare me off?"

"What? No!" He took his eyes off the road for a moment. "Of course not!"

Then he sighed, a heavy, weary sigh. "I talked to my friend Bran when we were still back in Nova Scotia. He told me I shouldn't blindside you with my family. That you should know what you're getting into. He's right. And maybe there's a part of me that thinks that maybe it'll help you understand me a little better, too." He looked over again, a grim smile on his lips. "Warts and all."

She tried a small smile. "Kissing frogs who turn into princes?"

"I'm no prince." He smiled back, though it was edged with tension. "Also, a holiday cocktail party means Mom will be on her best behavior, or at least I hope so. Tomorrow morning we'll drive back and it'll be over and done with."

They still hadn't talked about when she'd be returning home, but she did have to be back by

Thursday of the following week. She couldn't take unlimited vacation and leave Tom in the lurch with the hotel.

She supposed that meant in the new year she'd be talking to him about resigning and creating an exit plan.

The thought made her sad, and a bit lonely, but she was moving on to big things. And it would have to be done, regardless, because her maternity leave was scheduled to start at the beginning of April.

It was nearly eight when a gate swung open and they pulled into a large, circular drive. The lane leading up to the property was heavily treed, so Tori only saw darkness out the passenger side window. A number of cars were already parked. The party had begun, apparently.

"Cocktails now, dinner at eight thirty," he murmured, turning off the engine. "Phew. Are you ready?"

"No. You're making me nervous."

"I'm sorry." He ran his hand through his hair, a clear sign he was agitated. "I'm being a coward."

She turned in her seat. "Listen, we don't have to go in. If you're this upset, that tells me all I need to know. Don't do this because of me."

He relaxed a little. "I think it's like ripping off

a Band-Aid. Once it's done, I'll feel better. And then I won't have to worry about it again."

"Well, then, let's get ripping. It's going to get cold out here in about thirty seconds." A light snow had started to fall.

He got out and then went around the car to open her door, and held her elbow firmly as they walked to the entrance of the grand home.

At first glance, Tori thought the house was simply a large colonial style—gorgeous but not the imposing mansion she'd been expecting. But as they stepped up to the oversize oak door, she realized that tucked back behind the main house were expansive wings, afforded privacy by the large, sheltering trees to each side of the main building. "Oh," she whispered.

"Nine thousand square feet, give or take," he offered, knocking on the door.

Way larger than even the nicest house they'd looked at back home. And, if she could guess, well over twice the cost, especially when considering currency exchange.

She gripped her clutch even tighter.

The door opened and they were ushered in and divested of their outerwear; they walked only five feet when they were offered a cocktail. Jeremy accepted one while Tori said a quiet, "No, thank you."

Instead of leaving it there, though, Jeremy asked for them to bring her a club soda and lime.

"How did you know what I'd like?"

He leaned closer. "You've been drinking it all week at my place."

He noticed the most mundane things, and she couldn't help but be pleased.

Now they were at the door to a large room, and conversations hummed from inside. His mother was in there. Probably his sister. Stepfather. Their social circle. She was a small-town nobody from Nova Scotia. She couldn't be more out of place if she tried.

She was about to ask him for more time, but then a woman appeared at the door, carrying a glass of red wine, and smiled widely. "About time you got here! I wondered if you'd fed me to the wolves."

"Hey, Sarah." He gave her a hug, but it was more polite than overt affection. "I'd like you to meet Tori."

"Hello, Tori. Nice of you to…"

She'd just noticed Tori's baby bump. "Oh. *Oh.* Well. Congratulations."

Tori placed her hand protectively over the baby. "Thank you."

Sarah looked at Jeremy. "Does Mom know?"

"Of course not."

"Wow, Jeremy, you're going to make her a

grandmother. She won't be able to lie about her age anymore."

"Well, cheers to that." The siblings touched glasses.

Sarah relaxed a little. "Seriously, though, congratulations. I'm surprised as hell, but one of us deserves to be happy. When's the due date?"

"April fourteenth," Tori supplied.

"Well, you might as well come in. You can't stay in the doorway all night."

Tori's club soda arrived, so her hands were full of purse and drink as they entered a room that she was sure was nearly as big as her whole house.

The men wore black tie, the same as Jeremy, creating a striking look. The women were dressed in conservative cocktail dresses, with nary a bared shoulder or plunging neckline in sight. Except for one woman, Tori noticed. She had on a little black dress that dipped to the waist in the back, and came to mid-thigh. When she turned around, it was like looking at Sarah all over again, only twenty-five years older and with three times the amount of makeup.

Unless Tori was sadly mistaken, she'd also had substantial work done. Her face had a pinched look that wasn't quite natural.

The woman spied Jeremy and smiled, then her gaze lit on Tori, drifted down to her belly and moved back up with both surprise and distaste in their depths. *Here we go.*

At least the front of the dress was more appropriate than the back. She excused herself and came to stand in front of Jeremy, as if Tori wasn't there at all.

"So good of you to come, Jeremy."

"Mother." He leaned forward and kissed her cheek. Tori wasn't sure the kiss had even made contact with skin. "Merry Christmas. I'd like to introduce you to Victoria Sharpe."

Tori put down her drink and held out her hand. "Hello, Mrs...."

It struck her suddenly. Jeremy never mentioned his mother by her first name, and since she'd remarried her last name wouldn't be Fisher any longer. It would be something else. Something Tori didn't know. She wanted to sink through the floor, especially when the other woman made no move to reduce Tori's embarrassment. She didn't even shake her hand. Tori dropped her hand to her side, feeling sick to her stomach.

"Oh, I'm sorry, Tori. Mom is now Carol Heppner. I can't believe I forgot to mention that."

"Yes really, Jeremy, it's like you don't care who I am at all," his mother chided, but instead of being hurt she just looked...disinterested.

"Oh, wait." Tori tried a smile and pried open

the catch on her purse. "Mrs. Heppner, I brought you something. Just to say thank-you for having me tonight."

She took out the robin's-egg-blue bag and held it out. When she'd been shopping for Jeremy's decorations, she'd seen it and had thought maybe it would be fancy enough for his mother. She hadn't wanted to arrive empty-handed.

Jeremy looked uncomfortable and Carol stared at the bag for a moment before taking it. "Thank you."

She moved to hand it off to a servant when Jeremy's brittle voice came from beside her.

"Aren't you going to open it, Mother?"

With a sigh, Carol opened the bag, then the box inside, and the pouch inside that. She removed the delicate snowman on the red ribbon that Tori had thought so cute and that had taken a substantial chunk of her bank account.

"Isn't that…charming."

She stared at Tori's belly again, then looked at Jeremy and said, "I do hope you enjoy the party. Have you seen Sarah? She's here."

"We saw her on the way in." With a defiant set to his jaw, he added, "She wanted to congratulate us on the baby."

A weak smile touched his mother's lips. "Odd, how you wait until a party to tell your own mother. Oh, well. Let me add my congratulations, then. But excuse me. I do have other guests to attend to."

She walked away. Tori watched as she handed off the ornament to a staff member as if it were nothing at all.

"You got her a hostess gift? Tori, that's ballsy."

"Yeah, well, she didn't look impressed."

"Of course not. She's never impressed." His gaze softened.

"I knew she'd have…exacting tastes. I know it was small. And a snowman… I'm an idiot."

He put his arm around her. "No, you're not. You're incredibly sweet and have better manners than my mother. Come on, let's find Sarah. She's as emotionally stunted as the rest of us, but she tries. And she's an ally."

Tori tried not to laugh but couldn't help it. Emotionally stunted? She didn't think Jeremy was. She thought he covered a lot with smiles and charm, but the last week he'd revealed a lot about himself.

"All right. Could I have another club soda, though? I feel like I need to have something in my hand."

"Of course. And dinner will be soon."

They mingled their way through the room in search of Sarah, whom they found in a corner drinking a glass of wine and holding an animated conversation with a man who looked perhaps thirty. As they drew closer, Tori could tell the conversation was centered on financial stuff she didn't understand. Sarah was clearly schooling the younger man, who was openly flirting back. What was it like to have that kind of confidence?"

"Excuse me," Sarah said. "I'm going to chat with my brother for a few minutes."

She extricated herself from the conversation and turned to Tori and Jeremy. "Oh, my goodness. They get younger every time I turn around. Thanks for the rescue."

"One good turn deserves another. We saw Mom."

"That must have been entertaining. I'm sorry I missed it." She took a big sip of wine. "What did she say?"

Tori looked up. "She said congratulations."

Sarah snorted. "She did not. And if she did, it wasn't in that sweet way that you just did. By the way, I can't place your accent. Where are you from?"

"Nova Scotia."

Sarah looked at Jeremy. "Last summer's trip."

He grinned. "Surprise." Then he leaned over and kissed Tori's cheek. "It wasn't quite what we planned on happening, but life doesn't always go according to plan."

They chatted a while longer and Tori started

to relax. Once everyone was seated at dinner, she let out a long breath. "Okay. I think I'm doing okay."

"You are. I told you not to pay any attention to my mom. Everyone else loves you."

Well, everyone except Jeremy's stepdad. The best that could be said of him was that he was utterly ambivalent.

Tori and Jeremy sat together during the meal, which included foods that Tori had never even seen before but bravely tried. She avoided the pâté and soft cheese, but enjoyed whatever the poultry dish was—perhaps duck?—and some sort of fancy potato. And the dessert was delightful, a tarte tatin with cream. Not too exotic, but extra special. Something she'd love to have at the Sandpiper…

Except she wasn't going to be there anymore, was she? Her heart gave a little pang at the thought. Saying goodbye was going to be so very hard. She'd put her heart and soul into the resort.

As the sounds of clinking silverware and crystal glasses slowed, she wondered if this kind of thing would become her life. It was nice for a visit, but she wouldn't want to live like this. Then again, Jeremy didn't live like this. His place was extravagant but his mood was relaxed, his tastes plainer. Like eating casserole two hours late, or ordering in a pizza from his favorite pizza joint. Cheesecake at ten o'clock at night.

She understood now why he'd wanted her to come. This was where he'd come from, but it wasn't where he wanted to be. He'd always be connected to his family, but this wasn't the life he had chosen for himself.

Or for his child.

She leaned over. "This was delicious, but I think I get it now."

"Get what?"

"What you said about me needing to see it. Promise me we won't end up like this. I want backyard barbecues and kitchen parties and people feeling welcomed."

He looked into her eyes. "Of course you do. It's what you've always known."

"I'm sorry you haven't."

"I survived." He flashed her a smile. "Come on, let's go back to the drawing room, as Mother likes to call it. It makes her feel aristocratic."

She laughed and they rose from the table. Now that dinner was over, the mood was even more relaxed in the large room. More wine was poured, and brandy. Tori realized that Jeremy had had his cocktail upon entering and one glass of wine at dinner, but that was it. When she mentioned as much, he shrugged. "I know we said we'd stay the night and go back tomorrow morning, but now I'm thinking we can drive back tonight. If that's okay with you."

She had no desire to stay any longer than she had to. She was a fish out of water here. "Whatever you want to do."

"I'm going to find Mom and let her know. We don't have to stay much longer if you're tired."

He left her with Sarah, who was definitely staying as she'd now switched to gin and tonic. "I know, I shouldn't," she said. "But I am staying the night, and it's the only way these parties are bearable."

"Then why come?" Tori asked. She'd given up club soda and was now drinking straight-up water.

"I don't know. Because it's expected. Because we get the 'you only visit your mother twice a year' guilt trip. And because we can't stand each other, but a few times a year we pretend to and it makes us feel better about our stupid dysfunctional family."

Tori snorted. Sarah didn't have much of a filter after a few drinks.

"But you and Jeremy…you get along okay."

"We muddle through. Out of the whole family, we're probably the closest."

"I'm glad. He talks about you a lot."

Sarah looked pleased at that. "I think you're good for him, if tonight hasn't scared you off."

"We're trying to figure it out." She put her hand on her stomach and sighed. "Can you tell me where the powder room is? I haven't gone all night and the baby's sitting right in a good spot." She smiled at Sarah.

"Outside the door, go right, down the hall. There's a door on the left just across from Bruce's office." She turned up her nose. "He likes to go in there for a cigar after dinner. Gross."

"Thanks. If Jeremy comes back, tell him I won't be long."

She made her way down the hall, away from the noise. The house truly was gorgeous, a real showpiece with creamy walls, white trim and a gorgeous iron railing on the staircase leading to the next floor, which was now bedecked with boughs and ribbon. There wasn't a speck of dust or a thing out of place. No personal knick-knacks or photos; just perfectly placed flower arrangements—holiday themed, of course— and pieces of art on the walls. Each one was perfectly level, as if it wouldn't dare be a little bit crooked.

Beautiful, and perfect. But there was no personality, no sense of the people who lived there.

She caught sight of an open door—presumably the powder room—when she heard voices coming from the room across the hall.

Jeremy's voice. And his mother's in reply.

She went to the door, staying slightly behind. There'd been a strident reply to something from Jeremy, but she hadn't been able to make out the words. Now she strained to hear. She hoped he wasn't getting a lot of grief from his mother. They could just stay over if it was going to be a big deal for them to leave early.

"Why didn't I tell you before? When was the last time you called me, Mother? Asked how I was? I mean, do you even care?"

"Of course I care, Jeremy." Her voice was cold. "I'm going to be a grandmother."

"I highly doubt it. You weren't mother material, you sure as hell aren't cut out to be a grandmother."

Ouch.

"You're so cruel," she replied. "And finding out tonight, in a room full of guests? It was embarrassing. Or was that your intention?"

He didn't answer, so his mother continued in her patronizing voice. "Look, she's probably nice enough, in her way. But really, Jeremy? She's not our kind of people. She's plain, and…uncultured."

"And you know that after sneering at her for two minutes?"

"Seriously. The way you're acting, you'd think you were in love with the girl. You aren't, are you?"

Tori held her breath. Her pride stung from his mother's assessment, but she was angry on Jeremy's behalf. No wonder he stayed away. What a horrible creature.

Jeremy hesitated. Then he said the words: "Of course I'm not. Don't be ridiculous."

Tori's heart plummeted to her feet. The way he'd kissed her. Held her hand. Made love...

It couldn't all have been an act.

She refused to believe it.

"I'm not going to ask you how she got pregnant. We both know that and I don't need the details. What are you going to do about it now?"

"She's here, isn't she?" he snapped, and Tori blinked back tears. He sounded so...harsh. "Look. No kid of mine is going to wonder where the hell his father is. You and Dad...you should never have procreated. He left and you wanted nothing to do with us. And here's what you need to know. I will do anything—*anything*—to make sure I do a better job of parenting my kid than you ever did."

Silence dropped for a moment. Then his mother spoke quietly. "Even pretend to love its mother?"

"Even that. Whatever it takes."

"So you're not in love with her. I knew it."

"Mother, please."

Tori stepped backward from the door, reeling

from the pure derision laced in his voice. She hurried back down the hall, determined he not see her. She came across one of the waitstaff and asked where she could find another bathroom. Once she'd located it, she went inside, shut the door and sat on the closed toilet for thirty seconds while she tried to sort out her thoughts. Her feelings.

She'd been played.

Mother, please.

Those words replayed over and over in her head. She'd really fallen for it, hadn't she? All the expensive outings and private flights and sweet words… He'd used his money after all, to get her to do what he wanted. He didn't even have to get a lawyer involved. He'd used her emotions instead, and played her like a violin.

She got off the toilet, turned around and opened the lid. Though she hadn't thrown up for weeks now, her dinner came back up and left her gasping.

Then she flushed the toilet, washed her hands, and patted her face as best she could. She wouldn't cry, not now. But she was more than ready to go home and lick her wounds. And once she'd done that, she'd start making plans to raise her baby.

Hurt threatened to pierce her heart, but she steeled herself and kept it away by sheer force of will. She'd gone along with every single thing he'd suggested, and she'd fallen in love with him. Except it wasn't really him; just a show he'd put on to get what he wanted. And what made her the angriest was that he was planning on working out his childhood issues by using his own child as…what? Therapy? That was no way to bring a baby into the world. Not to solve your own problems.

She still had her clutch with her, and she took out her phone, turned on the data and booked a flight back to Halifax for the next day, on a commercial flight, which left approximately seventy-two dollars of available credit on her card. A knock sounded on the bathroom door just as she was getting the confirmation email. "Tori? Are you okay?"

"I'm fine," she replied, lifting her chin and staring at herself in the mirror. Right now she hated this dress. It wasn't her. It was someone she thought she could be. It was a lie, just like everything he'd said had been a lie.

"Are you sick?"

"I'll be right out." She squared her shoulders and opened the door, unprepared for the shaft of pain she felt upon seeing his concerned face. He wanted her baby, not her. And she rather wished he'd just been honest about that from the beginning, rather than manipulating her.

"Sorry. Turns out dinner didn't agree with me after all. I think I'd like to go…" She hesitated before saying home. "Back to the apartment."

He didn't say much, just watched her with an odd expression as she passed him on her way out the door and led the way to the stairs.

"If that's what you want, I'll get our coats."

It was a long drive back to the city. She didn't relish the idea of being in the car with him for that long, because she wasn't ready to talk about this yet. But it was her only way back to New York. It wasn't like she could ask Sarah. She'd been drinking all night. And Tori refused to cause a scene here.

She didn't bother saying goodbye to Sarah and she certainly didn't say goodbye to the hosts, who hadn't wanted her there to begin with. The snow flurries had stopped, thankfully, and at least they wouldn't be driving back in a heavier snowfall.

She got in the car and he turned on the heater while he cleared off the half inch or so of snow that had fallen earlier.

"Are you sure you're all right? You look flushed."

"I'm fine. Tired." Her heightened color was because she was agitated. Her heart ached and yet she felt outrage. At him, at herself for being so willing to fall for him and his pretty stories of what their life could be together.

She'd been a fool.

And yet she didn't know how to navigate the conversation that needed to happen, so she leaned her head against the car window and stared outside at the darkness. After a few minutes, she closed her eyes and pretended to sleep.

Her thoughts were anything but quiet.

Her heart was broken. Her trust was broken. Her faith was broken. She'd believed him when he'd said he cared for her. When he'd promised not to use his money to fight for his advantage. But he'd used it anyway, in a method far more ruthless.

He'd never said he loved her. He'd used the words *like* and *care*. But never *love*. It was as though his conscience wouldn't let him go that far.

Tears leaked from the corners of her eyes and she fought the urge to wipe them away.

Most of all she was angry with herself, for buying into it all so willingly.

He didn't say anything until they were in the city. "Tori, wake up. We're almost home."

She'd never been asleep but she pretended to perk up, sitting up in the seat and stretching. Her neck was cramped from leaning at an angle on the car door, and her heart felt raw and empty. Now she was minutes away from the conversation she didn't want to have. But she wouldn't run with her tail between her legs as if she had done something wrong.

"Feeling any better?"

"A little," she lied.

"The food was a little rich. Maybe it was just too much."

She didn't reply until they'd reached his building, gone up in the elevator and he was opening the door.

"It wasn't the food that made me sick." She peeled off the cape and put it on a chair in the foyer. She wouldn't take it with her. It was too expensive. A symbol of everything that was wrong with their relationship. She'd take only the things she'd brought with her in the first place. They were good enough for home.

"What was it?" Concern etched the corners of his eyes and she wanted to scream at him to stop pretending he cared.

"I was upset."

"I know it was a hard night—"

"I was upset at you." She kicked off her heels. "I heard you talking to your mother. And just so you know, I'm booked on a flight back home tomorrow morning. Leaving from Newark." It was the only direct flight she could manage, and she did not want to spend two hours in Toronto going through customs and sitting around waiting for another flight.

His face blanked, and a flush crept up his neck. "I don't know what you think you heard…"

Her anger flared now, hot and bright. "Please, do me the courtesy of not lying to my face again. I'm not mistaken. I have excellent hearing."

"My mother doesn't bring out my best qualities."

"Oh, you mean like finding out you're a liar? That you did exactly what you promised you wouldn't do?"

"I don't understand. Why are you yelling at me?"

Because you don't love me, she wanted to scream, but she could hardly do that. It sounded pitiful and she wasn't going to beg.

"It's okay that you're not in love with me. And yeah, we haven't known each other long, despite the fact that we're having a baby together. But you used me, and you pretended to care, because you'd do anything to ensure you show your mother what a horrible parent she was. Even pretend to love me. And those are your words, not mine."

His mouth fell open.

She waited.

"You weren't supposed to hear that," he said, his voice quiet and rough.

"Clearly. But I did hear it, and I'm glad. Because you manipulated me. Tell me, Jeremy, if you manipulate the mother of your child, are you going to manipulate the baby, too? Use him or her to work out all your own mommy and daddy issues?"

His cheeks reddened. "This is so easy for you to say, when you had two parents growing up who clearly loved and cared for you."

Tori took a step forward. "You are a grown man. Do not blame your poor decision-making on your mother. You had the chance to act with integrity. This is on you, and not anyone else." Tears burned in her eyes. "You used my emotions. But more than that, you've lost my respect. And that hurts almost as much as knowing you played me."

His face twisted in pain, and he turned away for a moment. She saw his shoulders rise and fall with a deep breath. Then he turned back. She didn't want to be moved by the look in his eyes. He looked tortured, but she steeled her spine. If he was, it was because he was dealing with the consequences of his actions.

"You've got it all wrong."

"How do I have it wrong? I heard you. Clear as day."

"I lied."

Her traitorous heart kicked a little bit when he said it, but she quickly replaced the momentary elation with doubt. "You lied…to whom?

To me? To your mother? How am I supposed to believe you?"

Jeremy ran his hand through his hair, a gesture she now knew he used when he was agitated. "To my mother. Do you seriously think that I would admit my feelings for you to her?"

"Why not? What would happen if you did? It's not like you have a great relationship with her anyway."

"I just... I keep my feelings locked away there. Anytime I tried to talk to her as a kid I was told to get over it or I got a laundry list of all the advantages I had and how I was ungrateful for complaining. It's what I do, on instinct. So does Sarah. We all do." He lowered his voice. "I don't... I mean, it's a vulnerability thing."

She could understand that, but it didn't excuse his behavior. "Again, Jeremy, you're a grown man. You're educated, successful. Powerful. And you can't stand up to your mom? That says a lot to me."

"I don't want her to know how I feel. I don't want her to see any weakness. My feelings for you—"

"What, make you weak?" Hardly a compliment. "When people care about each other, it's supposed to make them *more*, not *less*. And somehow you've got it in your brain that weakness, vulnerability, is a bad thing. It's not."

"It's never been a good thing," he bit back. "For Pete's sake, I don't even think I know how to love anyone. This whole situation terrifies me."

Everything was falling apart. Even if it was true that he'd lied to his mom, that he really did care about her, he considered that a chink in his armor.

She wanted to believe his feelings for her were real. But even if they were, tonight had cast serious doubts on their future. If he was incapable of loving, if he considered that a weakness, how could he possibly love their baby? For all his good intentions, she never wanted her child to feel rejected by its father. Or to have to beg for affection.

"Let me tell you about weakness," she said quietly. "And vulnerability. From the moment I discovered I was pregnant, I knew I was vulnerable because of the power imbalance in our situations. I wouldn't have the resources to fight you for custody of our child if you decided to take me to court. Then you showed up and I was forced to tell you the truth. I figured if we could be on good terms, we could work through something together. You reminded me of the man I met in the summer. You were kind. I started to care for you again. You asked me to come here, and I did. You asked me to uproot my life and I was willing to consider it, even though the job I love and my family and friends are all back in Nova Scotia. I trusted you. I believed in you. And I'm not afraid to say it, even though you are. I fell in love with you."

"Tori—"

"No." She held up a hand. "Just no. I fell in love with the person I thought Jeremy Fisher was. Tonight I discovered he is someone else. He did a great job of faking it, but I don't know you. You wanted me to go tonight so I knew what I was getting into, and boy do I ever. So I'm going home. And after a while, we'll discuss custody and visitation like rational adults, I hope. Financial situation or not, I will fight back if you choose to get lawyers involved. I hope it doesn't come to that."

His eyes dulled and he looked utterly bereft. She didn't want to be affected by his forlorn look, but she was.

"Everything before tonight… It was true. I swear it."

Her insides trembled. "I don't know how to believe you. I don't know which Jeremy is the real one. And that's not something I'm willing to bet my life or my baby's happiness on. I'm sorry, Jeremy."

She moved past him and down the hall to her room, where she started to pack her bags. He came to stand in the doorway. "Please, Tori. I'm trying here." He ran his hand through his hair. "My mom brings out the worst in me, and I'm so sorry. I should have been stronger. Should have been honest."

She looked up at him. "The thing is, I think you were honest. I think your number one priority is to show your mother that you can be better than her. It's not me, and it's not love that's driving that decision. I won't uproot my whole life on that sort of gamble."

For a moment, she thought she saw tears glimmer in his eyes, and her resolve wavered. Then he swallowed and said, "What time is your flight tomorrow?"

"Ten."

"Get some sleep, then. I'll get you to the airport in lots of time."

She opened a drawer and took out some sweaters.

"Tori, I'm sorry. I handled everything badly. I know I messed this up. Wait, and let's try to work through it."

"I just need to go home," she said, not looking at him.

She sensed when he left her doorway, and she braced her hands on her suitcase as her head drooped. Was she overreacting? His explanations made sense, but the fact remained that even if he'd lied to his mother, he hadn't stood up for

Tori. And even though he'd said he'd lied, he hadn't said that he loved her, either. Even after she'd admitted her feelings first.

She texted her mom, asking if she could pick her up at the airport the next afternoon, then finished packing. She sat up the rest of the night, unable to sleep.

When six thirty rolled around, she ordered a taxi and quietly made her way out of his apartment and to the bottom floor. She couldn't handle saying goodbye; her feelings were too raw. She didn't want to sit through another ride to the airport, either. When the cab arrived, the driver put her suitcase and carry bag in the trunk and they were off to New Jersey.

She was going home. Alone.

CHAPTER FOURTEEN

SHE WAS GONE.

Jeremy stared at the spare room with disbelief. She'd run. Granted, last night had been a disaster. But he would have taken her to the airport. He'd hoped that they'd get up this morning and be able to talk about what had happened without the high emotions of last night. Maybe even change her mind.

But she was gone.

He wandered to the main living area, his heart sore. The flower arrangement she'd bought was still on the dining table; the evergreen centerpiece in the living room, along with that silly little tree. A few dishes remained in the sink from where they'd had a cup of coffee yesterday afternoon before heading to Connecticut.

She was still here, whether he wanted her to be or not.

Jeremy wandered to the windows and looked out over the snowy city. She'd been right about pretty much everything. He should have stood up to his mother. Why not? It wasn't as if they had a relationship to speak of anyway. But that house… Anytime he was inside he was back to being that little boy again. Protecting himself and his feelings against ridicule and neglect. Poor little rich boy.

He knew very well that rich people could be miserable, too.

It was eight o'clock now. She'd be boarding in an hour, heading back to Nova Scotia and the family and job she loved. After yesterday, he had no right to take her away from that. No matter how much he'd really wanted to try for the life they'd begun to plan.

And his baby… He sank onto the sofa and put his head in his hands. No matter what she thought of him, he wouldn't put either of them through a legal battle. And there was no way he'd take the baby from her. She was going to be a damned good mother.

He wandered through the day aimlessly. Sarah called on her way back from Connecticut and he put her off. Cole texted and he didn't reply. Right now he was licking his wounds.

If only she hadn't heard him in Bruce's office. He could have kept his mom at arm's length and then gone on with his plans. And yet, deep down, he knew that was a coward's reasoning.

He'd been fighting his feelings all week. He'd

kept telling himself that he wasn't capable of love. That it wasn't on his agenda. That it wasn't necessary for them to make this work.

But he'd been lying to himself. He did love her. Maybe he had from the beginning, when their connection had been so strong it had knocked him off his feet. When he'd looked for a reason to go back and see her again. Bringing her here to New York.

Making love.

It had been love, too. Not just sex. He just hadn't wanted to admit it because it scared the hell out of him. Love was a weakness that could be exploited.

Except Tori would never do that. He knew that in his heart, and he'd lied to himself until it was too late and she had walked away.

And he could tell her all of that, but she was right. She didn't know which version was true, and she couldn't uproot her life for someone she didn't trust.

She'd loved him. She'd said it. And he'd messed it up by denying what was right in front of his face.

He sat on the sofa until the light turned dark again.

Arrivals seemed to take forever. First, she was seated at the very back of the plane, which meant she was last to get off. Then there was the long walk to customs, and the line to get through. Then waiting for luggage. Finally she cleared the secure area and walked through the doors to see her mom waiting, a smile on her face.

Tori started to cry.

"Oh, honey!" Shelley came forward and gave her a big, reassuring hug while Tori's hand clung to the handle of her suitcase. "Come on. Let's get you to the car and you can tell me what happened."

She had never been so glad to see someone in her whole life.

It took only a few minutes to reach the car in the parking garage and head out onto the highway that would take them first into Halifax, and then down to the South Shore. For the first few minutes, Shelley simply reached over and patted Tori's hand, as if to say, *It's going to be okay.* She kept quiet for ten minutes or so, and then simply said, "So what went wrong?"

Tori sighed. "I don't know where to start."

"Then let's stop somewhere to eat. Neither of us has had lunch. Did you even have breakfast?"

She shrugged. "I had a yogurt at the airport."

"Where do you want to go?"

"I don't care."

Shelley quieted again, and then turned off the highway and drove to a diner in Bedford. "Quieter here than Cora's on a Sunday," she said. "And breakfast all day. Come on."

She wasn't feeling very hungry, but she ordered a breakfast skillet anyway, to make her mom happy. And orange juice, because it was her favorite.

Once they'd placed their orders, Shelley looked at her with a "tell your mom about it" expression. "Okay. So you came back a few days early, looking like a whipped puppy. What happened?"

She told her mom everything. By the time she finished, their meals had been placed in front of them and Shelley had gotten a refill of her coffee.

"Baby girl," she said, on a sigh. "You're right. You deserve a man who will stand up for you, and for your family. Who will do the right thing."

"I thought he was that man, you know? That's what hurts so much." She picked at a chunk of hash-browned potato in her skillet.

"You think he was pretending the whole time?"

Her fork kept moving the piece of potato around and around. "I did when I first heard what he said. And then… Oh, Mom. I don't know. It's hard to believe that it wasn't real. The whole week was actually pretty magical. And when he heard the baby's heartbeat…"

"You wonder how he could be such a good actor?"

"I…yeah. And I get mad at myself for wanting

to believe him. But he never said he loves me. I keep coming back to that. And the fact that I don't know if I could believe him even if he did say it."

She sniffled. Put down her fork. "He had a rotten childhood. He never had a solid family unit like I had with you and Dad."

"Does that excuse his behavior?"

She shook her head. "But it makes me understand it. I know he wants to be a good father, but what if he just doesn't have the ability to let himself love someone? I thought I could go through with it. We were getting along so well. I could see our relationship growing so that someday maybe it would be...whole."

"But..."

"But it would never be what you had with Dad. And I don't want to settle for anything less."

Shelley reached for her napkin and dabbed her eyes and her nose. "Well, I guess your dad and I did something right."

"I miss him."

"Me, too, honey. Every day."

They picked at their food. Tori was hungry, and the more she ate, the better she felt. Even though she couldn't finish the large portion, she'd needed the nutrition. So did the baby.

Shelley looked up at her. "You said before that you thought you could go through with it. Don't hate me for asking, but is there a chance you're using what happened as a way out?"

She wanted to say yes without hesitation, but she couldn't.

"You hesitated, which means you're thinking about it. I just think maybe Jeremy isn't the villain he's been made out to be. Yes, he made a mistake and you absolutely deserve better. You shouldn't settle for less. But you need to be clear on your own motives too, sweetie. Picking up and moving countries to be with a man you care about but who might not love you in return is a big risk."

The meal she'd just eaten churned in her stomach. "And he gave me a way out without me having to take any responsibility." Ugh, had she really done that? Used his weakness to justify her own behavior, her own fears?

"I'm not saying you should have stayed. I think I'm saying this is a big mess, and the only way through it is for both of you to be completely honest with each other. You reacted and you left. But now there are a lot of feelings to sort through. I think you should take the time to do it." Then Shelley smiled. "And you can spend Christmas with your mama while you're sorting things out."

"I love you, Mom."

Shelley reached for the bill. "Well, duh. Of course you do. Look, kiddo, since your dad died,

I've watched you be afraid. It made you grow up in a hurry. You haven't had a lot of relationships since Riley broke your trust, and I think that trust is your deal breaker. Have you told Jeremy that?"

"Not really."

"Look, your dad set a wonderful example and standard, but you were also hurt when he left."

"He didn't leave us. Not like Jeremy's dad did."

"Not in the same way, but he left just the same. Don't be afraid to love someone, honey. Jeremy lied to his mom. He didn't stand up for you. But that doesn't mean he doesn't love you."

"He didn't say it."

"I know. Just give it some thought, and when you're ready, you and Jeremy need to talk. Even if it's just to decide what's going to happen with visitation."

They got up and Shelley paid the bill, and then they got on the road again. As they merged onto the highway, Tori sighed. "I keep telling myself I'm afraid he'll use his money and power to take the baby. I feel like I need to protect myself and prepare for that possibility. And then my heart says he would never do such a thing. And I think I'm being a fool, again."

Shelley didn't answer, but Tori knew exactly what she would say. Sit on it. Think about it and sort through her feelings. And then talk to Jeremy.

* * *

The bar was crowded and noisy, and Jeremy could tell Bran was only going through the motions. Cole, on the other hand, was flirting with their waitress and being his charming self. And Jeremy was running around with his tail between his legs.

Still. He couldn't mope around his apartment forever, and Bran needed to get out now and again. His possession date for the new house was the first of February; then the three of them hanging out would be a rare occasion.

Of course, Bran was going to be close to Tori. And that irritated Jeremy like a scratchy tag on the back of his neck.

"Beer, whiskey, and a rum and coke." The waitress put their drinks on the table. "Can I get you anything else?"

"We're good for now," Cole said, flashing her a million-dollar smile.

She smiled back and was gone with a twitch of her hip.

"Stop that," Bran said, scowling. "You're not twenty-five anymore, Cole."

"What? The day I stop flirting is the day I die."

Bran shook his head. "Yeah, but you have no follow-through. You work too much."

Jeremy shook his head. "Listen, you two, I came out for drinks and a good time."

Cole sipped on his rum and coke. "No, you didn't. You came out because you're being a sad sack since Tori went back to Canada. We don't need to tell you how you messed that up, Jer."

He took a big pull of his beer. "Yeah, sure. I know that."

Bran looked at him. "When we saw you in your office that day, you looked pretty happy. She thinks you were faking it, right? That she was manipulated? But was she?"

The beer didn't quite settle in his stomach. "Of course not. I mean, I wanted to bring her around, but damn, you know?" He scowled. "The way I sounded at my mom's... It was like she wasn't worth loving. I don't blame her for being furious. Or walking away."

Cole saluted with his glass. "Well done, dumbass."

Bran rolled his eyes. "Jer, let me ask you this. What was the moment you first knew?"

"First knew what?"

"That you loved her."

The table went silent.

Bran took a drink of his whiskey and pushed back his shaggy hair. "Look, when I met Becca, I didn't love her at first. But there was a moment. It wasn't even a big moment. She was in my place and she looked over her shoulder at me and laughed and it was just there. *Bam, I love her.*

And I'm guessing you had that moment, because you've been dragging yourself around for the last five days, beating yourself up and thinking about nothing but the fact she's gone. So when was it?"

Jeremy's throat tightened. "When we were skating. She did this turn thing and faced me, holding my hands, and she laughed and had this weird hat on with her ponytail out the top, and it was like someone opened my heart and poured in a ray of sunshine."

Cole swore and shook his head.

Bran wagged a finger at him. "Look, he-man. Don't be like that just because it hasn't happened to you."

Then Bran turned to Jeremy. "Dude, I'm telling you right now. You've got to go make this right. I won't have another chance with Becca. She's gone, but Tori isn't. She needs to know how you feel. You've got to lay it on the line, brother. You'll regret it forever if you don't. And she's having your kid. If you want to have a relationship with him or her, if you want to do better than your own father did, you've got to step up."

"She doesn't want to see me."

"Bull. I'm telling you right now, there's no room for pride at this point. You might have to beg. But if you love her…"

"Of course I do. And my kid, too. Hearing that heartbeat…"

"Then fight for her. You didn't do that when you had the chance, don't you see? And if she loves you, too, that had to break her heart."

Cole took a long drink. "As much as it pains me to say it, I agree with Dear Abby here. We were with you at school. We know you almost as well as you know yourself. You would do anything to not be your dad, and that's great. So stop acting like him. Man, every time you go to that house you act like… I don't know. Like she has some kind of say over your life. You're a grown man."

Jeremy chuckled despite the sting he felt at Cole's words. "That's what Tori said."

"So quit running away and stand up to your mom instead of all that polite-distance kind of thing. And go talk to Tori. Tell her how you feel."

"Sometimes manning up means laying your heart on the line, rather than being 'strong,' you know?" Bran finished his whiskey. "I'm telling you guys, I'm a freaking mess, but I wouldn't trade any of the time I had with Bec."

"We know, man." Jeremy put his hand on Bran's shoulder. "And you're right. I just… I don't know how to do this."

Cole leaned forward. "I think the correct word is *beg*. Or maybe *grovel*."

"Helpful," Jeremy muttered. "I guess…family means everything to Tori. She loves her mom so

much, and her dad died a couple years ago, and…
I feel like a horrible human, not feeling that kind
of connection or loyalty to my own family. Sarah
excluded."

"Hey." Bran looked him dead in the eye. "Family is more than genetics. We learned that at Merrick."

"Go Monarchs," Cole and Jeremy said, lifting
their glasses.

Jeremy settled back into his chair, while Cole
signaled for another round. "Yeah, you're right.
You guys are my brothers."

"And it's our job to kick you when you're being
an idiot. So get yourself together and figure out
how you're going to get her back. It's Christmas.
A good present should come with the groveling."

The next round of drinks appeared, and Jeremy perked up. He at least had to try. He'd been
miserable the last few days. The apartment was
cold and empty. He couldn't focus. He stared endlessly at the ultrasound picture. He'd let the best
thing in his life get away, because he couldn't
deal with his feelings.

And as Bran and Cole started to discuss ordering some snacks, Jeremy got the first inklings of
a plan. Starting tomorrow, he'd have to get himself in gear in order to have it all set for Christmas.

CHAPTER FIFTEEN

CHRISTMAS MORNING DAWNED bright and clear, with a pristine blue sky and a new dusting of snow that made everything look fresh and white but didn't play havoc with road conditions. Tori had slept at her mom's, and would stop in at the Sandpiper later. They kept a very light staff on Christmas Day and Boxing Day, and they had minimal bookings, too. Still, essential staff were away from their loved ones on Christmas morning, so she'd arranged for them all to have breakfast midmorning. The crew would have breakfast meats and eggs cooked by Neil and his sous chefs, and she'd brought in pastries from a local bakery. She'd even made a huge bowl of fruit salad herself and left it in the massive fridge.

Now, though, at barely eight o'clock, she sat beside her mother's decorated spruce tree, looking at the arrangement of presents beneath it.

She had a lot to be thankful for. She was healthy, her baby was healthy, she had a job she loved and a mother who doted on her. And yet the holiday felt lusterless and underwhelming. All because she couldn't get the father of her child off her mind.

"I made you tea," Shelley said, coming in from the kitchen. They were both dressed in fuzzy new pajamas; getting new ones on Christmas Eve had been a tradition for her when she was a kid, and in the past few years they'd taken to buying them for each other. She handed Tori the cup and sat down on a footstool nearby, cradling her own cup of coffee. "So. Have you opened your stocking?"

"I was waiting for you."

"Let me turn on some Christmas music first."

With the sound of carols in the background and the lights on the tree turned on, Tori reached for her stocking. Inside was her favorite chocolate, a three-pack of maternity underwear, some soft and fuzzy socks and the usual toiletries—body wash, deodorant, shampoo. There were some treats, too, like a new kind of tea and a little box of mini-facials. "Mom, this was too much."

"Don't be silly." Shelley was opening her own stocking, with her favorite treats and beauty brands, as well.

There were only a few presents under the tree. Two for each of them from each other, and there was one from the staff for Tori and one from the other nurses on Shelley's unit. Tori oohed over a new maternity outfit in the first box, and then watched as her mom opened her new pressure cooker she'd asked for. Her second gift contained a gorgeous lemon-yellow crocheted blanket.

"Oh, Mom."

"I haven't crocheted in years, but I figured this was as good a time as any to get out the old hook and take it up again. Do you like it?"

Tori ran her hand over the soft, fine yarn. "I love it. The baby will love it, too, because Grandma made it."

"Merry Christmas, sweetie."

"Open your last one, Mom."

She handed the gift bag to her mom. Shelley reached inside and took out a small box, then opened the box and withdrew the Christmas ornament. It was a glass ball with white and gold and the word *Grandma* painted on it with glitter.

"Where in the world did you find this?"

"In a little shop in New York." She had a similar ornament still tucked away in a drawer in her room. The one she'd bought for Jeremy but had forgotten to give him. She'd grabbed it at the last minute and put it in her luggage, hoping it would make the trip without breaking.

She'd been so excited that day. And that night, she and Jeremy had slept together.

"Are you okay?"

"I'm fine." She put on a smile. "Really. We're

both fine." She put her hand on her tummy. "And hungry."

They'd picked up the paper from their gifts and were just heading to the kitchen when there was a knock on the door.

"You expecting someone?" Tori called, as she opened the fridge door and got out eggs and ham for omelets.

When there was no answer right away, she straightened and poked her head out of the kitchen. "Who is it?"

Jeremy stepped into the entryway. "It's me."

She shouldn't be so glad to see him. But she was. He was here. In Nova Scotia. In her mother's hall. On Christmas morning.

"Hi," she said, belatedly realizing she was dressed in penguin pajamas with slippers on her feet and her hair in a messy ponytail.

"Merry Christmas."

It was incredibly awkward and emotionally charged. Shelley took a step back and murmured, "I'll just go start breakfast," while Tori and Jeremy stared at each other for a long, painful moment.

"You look wonderful," he said, his voice soft, and she wanted to believe him so badly it hurt.

"What are you doing here?"

"I came to ask for your forgiveness." He stepped forward but only to the edge of the mat;

a film of snow was on his shoes. She went to him instead, not necessarily for intimacy but more for privacy. Her mother's house wasn't large, and conversations were easily overheard. She laughed a little as Shelley made an inordinate amount of noise with frying pans.

"You look like your mom," he said gently. "She frowns like you, too. Told me I'd better get it right this time."

Tori's cheeks heated. "Mom doesn't mince words."

"Neither does her daughter. And I've recently discovered that both of you are pretty much right."

She didn't want to hope. But it was Christmas. And he looked so handsome in perfectly fitted jeans and his peacoat, his hair slightly mussed and his gray eyes focused on her so intently.

His gaze swept down to her belly and back up. "You're feeling okay?"

She nodded, her throat tightening. "Yeah, we're both okay. The baby's been moving around a lot."

"That's good."

"Yeah."

"Tori—" His voice broke off, and then he took a breath and squared his shoulders. "I went to see my mother. And I told her what I should have told her the night of the party. I told her that I love you, and I love this baby, and that I want to do right by both of you. And I owe you such a huge apology, Tori. I never showed my emotions. Not in that house, not with any of my relationships, because every time I did I got punished for it. But you invited me to. You gave me a safe place with no judgment and I used that gift to hurt you. I'm so sorry, Tori. More than you know."

She stood there dumbly, not knowing what to say or do. It scared her how much she wanted to believe him. She'd had time to think over the past several days, and really look at what had happened. He'd hurt her terribly at the party, while she'd still been stinging from his mother's cold reception. And she'd felt incredibly out of her depth. And no, he hadn't told her that he loved her, but he had tried to explain and she hadn't let him.

Because she, too, was scared. And she'd run.

"You love me?" she asked. "And the baby? Not just so that we won't be in separate countries or living in separate homes?"

He swallowed. "I loved this baby from the moment I saw that picture on the ultrasound machine. And I think I loved you all along. But Tori, your family is here. Your job is here. I won't ask you to leave that behind, not if you don't want to."

"And I will stay here, and you'll stay…"

His gray eyes softened. "In New York. We'll work this out on your terms, Tori. I can't force you to forgive me, or love me. But you're going to be a wonderful mother, and I think the best way for me to be a good dad is to make sure you're happy."

Her eyes stung as tears sprang into them. "But you said you love me."

He nodded, and his eyes were bright, too. "I do. Enough to let you go, if that's what you want."

She caught her breath, and it sounded almost like a sob, but she wouldn't let that happen. She wouldn't cry today. "What if that's not what I want?"

The air between them stilled. "Then come over here and put me out of my misery."

She took three halting steps and then threw herself into his arms. His tightened around her, holding her close, the baby sandwiched between them. "You feel good," he whispered in her ear. "I was sure you'd tell me to walk out. Thank you for not doing that."

She nodded against his coat and sniffed. "It's partly my fault, too. I was overwhelmed and feeling like someone's poor cousin, and I wanted you to stand up for me. When you didn't… I just wanted to go home, where it was familiar. I used your mistake as an excuse, rather than talking it out. And I ran away."

"You had good reason. But, sweetheart…" His breath was warm against her ear. "I made a mistake. I didn't stop loving you. I just was too afraid to say it. Loving people has always made me weak, so I told myself I was incapable of it." He pushed back a little so he could look into her eyes. "Until now."

And then he kissed her, a wild welcoming that seemed to put everything right that had gone wrong. It wasn't the kiss of a coward or a pretender; it was the kiss of a man claiming the woman he loved. And when his hand cradled her baby bump, she closed her eyes and let the bit of gratitude that had been missing this morning trickle in.

"I hate to break up this happy reunion, but I have ham and cheese omelets and home fries for anyone who's hungry. That includes you, Jeremy."

He looked into Tori's eyes. "I don't deserve that kind of welcome," he whispered.

"Don't be silly. This is how family works." She clasped his hand. "We mess up and we forgive each other. I was awfully lonely this morning, Jeremy. Wishing you were here. Wondering if I should call you and what I should say. I'd forgiven you for what happened at the party, but I was still afraid, you see."

"You were gone about ten minutes before I started missing you," he murmured, kissing her forehead. "And my real brothers—Cole and

Bran—told me I was an idiot for blowing it. It has to be love," he continued, squeezing her fingers. "Nothing else could ever hurt me this much."

Considering the pain he'd been through as a boy, that was saying something. And what was more, she believed him. Because the Jeremy at the party wasn't the real Jeremy. She'd had time to think about that and realize that she'd let one five-minute conversation negate everything else between them. The Jeremy in all the other moments was the real man. And he was something special.

"Let's have breakfast, then."

"Okay. And then I want you to get dressed, because I have something to show you."

"You do?"

"A surprise."

"You and your surprises," she said, making a *tsk* sound. But as they walked to the kitchen, Christmas was suddenly very merry indeed.

While Tori was having a quick shower and getting dressed, Jeremy grabbed a dish towel and started drying dishes for Shelley.

"Mrs. Sharpe?"

She looked up at him, her hands in the dishwater. "You'd better call me Shelley, don't you think?"

"Maybe another time. Right now... Well, since Tori's dad isn't here, I'm going to ask you."

She reached for the dish towel in his hands and dried hers off, then looked up at him. "Ask me what?"

His stomach quivered. This emotional nakedness was all new to him, and he was terrified he was going to get a lecture once he said what he needed to say. But it was the right thing to do.

"Ask you for permission to marry your daughter."

Her gaze bored into him, and he couldn't tell what she was thinking. After what had happened, he rather expected he was being measured and coming up short.

"My girl can make up her own mind."

He nodded. "Yes, she can. But your family is different from mine, and your approval means a lot. So I'm asking anyway."

Her expression softened. "If Tori says yes, I certainly won't stand in her way."

He sagged with relief. "Okay. Phew. Thanks for not giving me the third degree."

She touched his arm. "Look. Clearly I don't have to worry about her materially, her or the baby. My biggest concern is for her heart. I saw her face when she realized it was you at the door, and I saw yours, too. There's far more between you than just a baby. So I'll leave you two to work out whatever future fits."

"Even if I take her away?"

She nodded. "Even then."

"Mrs. Sharpe?"

"Shelley. And yes?"

"I wish I'd had a mom like you."

To his surprise, she handed him back the dish towel and patted his arm. "Well, now you do."

She went back to washing dishes as if she hadn't just turned his world on its end.

When Tori came back to the kitchen, he and Shelley were talking about Sharpe Christmas traditions. He broke off midsentence when Tori appeared in the doorway. She wore a new outfit of navy leggings and a soft gray sweater that molded to her shape and made her look so beautiful and maternal he thought his heart might burst. "Look at you," he said, putting down the towel.

"It's new. From Mom, for Christmas." She turned in a circle. "See, Mom? Fits perfectly."

"You look lovely." Shelley let the water out of the sink. "Now go on. Jeremy has a surprise for you. I'll expect you back for dinner at five."

"We'll be back before then," Jeremy assured her. "You shouldn't have to cook a whole Christmas dinner yourself."

"Take your time," she said with a laugh. "The prep's done. I'm going to put the bird in the oven and have a nap. Maybe read one of the books I got from the girls at work."

He held Tori's coat for her—still the parka that

needed replacing—and then took her hand, leading her to his rented car. "Did you stay at the inn?" she asked, waiting as he opened the door for her.

"No, here in Lunenburg. I didn't want you to know I was in town yet."

"Oh."

"Come on. I've got something to show you."

They drove past Liverpool and toward the Sandpiper, and then past it. He looked over at her face as he turned up the lane leading to the house on the beach, the one they'd looked at after their feed of fish and chips. Her eyes widened.

"What are we doing here?"

"You'll see."

The gate was open, and they drove through, up the drive to the house. A huge wreath was on the front door, and just like at her mom's, a light dusting of snow made everything postcard perfect. He parked and got out of the car, patted his pocket, and went around to open her door. She put her hand in his and got out.

"Jeremy?"

"Come on."

He led her to the bluff overlooking the private stretch of beach. The wind was brisk off the water, but not bitter. The caps were white and the faint sound of the breakers touched his ears. This had been the right choice. No question.

"Tori?"

"Yes?"

"Remember the night we watched *Miracle on 34th Street*?"

She nodded.

"And there was the scene, at the end of the date, where Bryan proposes and she turns him down?"

Tori's eyes widened as she turned away from the ocean and stared up at him. "What?"

It was now or never. "You said to me, I don't know why she's so mean to Bryan. And I said, because she's scared. Plus they had to work to get to their happy ending."

She nodded, just barely, and he reached inside his pocket. "I know you're scared. I'm scared. But we shouldn't let that stop us from being happy. Not if we can be scared together. I'm ready to work toward that happy ending if you are."

And he held out the red ring box, identical to the one in the movie, and opened it.

Tori stared at the ring. It was possibly the most gorgeous thing she'd ever seen, nestled in velvet, winking in the winter sunlight. "You're proposing?"

"I am. I even asked your mom for permission."

She choked out a laugh, imagining how that conversation must have gone. "Oh, you didn't."

"I did. Because while my family is a hot

mess, yours isn't. I thought it would mean a lot to you."

She sighed. "It does."

"Tori?"

She couldn't stop staring at the ring. "Hmm?"

"Will you marry me?"

She looked up at him, all gray stormy eyes and wild hair and sexy vulnerability. It was hard to believe that a chance affair months earlier had led to this moment, but it had, and he was standing before her, asking her to be his wife.

And she knew now, without a doubt, that he'd lied to his mom and he'd been honest every step of the way. The proof was in his smiles, in his tender gestures, in the way he made her laugh. In the way they made love. He wasn't perfect. And neither was she. But he was hers, and she was his, and it was time she had a little faith.

So she nodded, said yes, and told him to put it on her finger.

When he slid it over her knuckle, she started to cry. It was beautiful, but what it meant was more so. They'd stopped being afraid and had started facing things together.

He kissed her softly, his lips cold from the wind. "So that's not the only surprise," he said against her mouth.

"It's not?"

"Don't you wonder why I brought you here?"

She looked around. The for-sale sign was gone from the yard. There was a wreath on the door. "I don't know, but don't you think the owners will wonder why we're standing out here on their bluff?"

He reached into his pocket again, and this time he took out a key and placed it in her palm.

She lifted startled eyes to his.

"I doubt it, since I'm the new owner."

"You... What?"

He grinned at her now, excitement flashing through his smile. "You love it here. I love it here. I don't necessarily want to relocate, but can you think of a better summer home? You can be close to your mom whenever you want. We can spend summer days building sandcastles with our kids on the beach. We can put a boat in here and sail down the coast. Have bonfires in the back. Marrying me shouldn't have to mean you leave home behind. Not when we can manage to have you here. And if you want to keep up with your innkeeper roots..." He swept his arm to the other side of the property. "The guesthouse is there. You're right. You could turn it into a vacation rental with no trouble at all. If you want to."

She couldn't believe it. "You bought me...a house? For Christmas?"

He nodded.

She started to laugh. And then she laughed

more and more until the sound of it echoed through the winter air.

"What's so funny?" His brows pulled together.

"Just that when we were looking at houses, you said this one wasn't large enough to suit. And now it's yours."

"I said it wasn't suited for Bran. Me? Well, I realized that it's not the house but the love inside it that matters." He spread his arms wide. "I came from a huge mansion with every advantage, but little love. Honey, let me tell you, this house is plenty big enough, as long as you're inside it."

She wrapped her arms around him and hugged him tight. She wasn't sure if fate was a thing, or serendipity, or what, but something had brought him here last summer and turned her world upside down. It was wonderful.

"Let's go inside," she suggested.

"You've got the key."

She went up the walk and turned the lock easily. Inside smelled like pine cones and cinnamon. There was no furniture, but in the corner of the living room, by the fireplace, was a huge decorated tree.

"Merry Christmas, sweetheart," he said from behind her.

She spun in a circle. "It really is. And now is the perfect time to give you your present."

She loved the look on his face right now. He'd

thought he'd been in charge of all the surprises today, but she had one more.

"But you didn't even know you were going to see me."

She reached into her handbag and took out the little gift bag she'd hidden in his apartment. The one that had made it through without getting crushed in her luggage, despite being hastily shoved inside without soft packing to keep it safe. And before this Christmas tree was the perfect moment. She handed it to him and smiled. "Merry Christmas, Jeremy."

She stood back while he removed the tissue, then reached inside. The little box was the same as her mom's had been, but what was inside was even more special.

He opened the lid and took out the ornament she'd bought.

It was white, too, but in pink glitter it spelled out "Daddy's Girl" in swooping cursive.

His gaze shot up to hers. "Daddy's girl... We're having a girl?"

She nodded, tears clogging her throat. The look on his face right now... It was almost the same as when she'd first told him about the baby. Terror and surprise but now with an added ingredient: joy.

"I found out a bit by accident, just before we left for New York. I was going to tell you the night I'd decorated your apartment, but then we kind of fought and then we made up and it wasn't the right moment. But now…now it's right. We're having a baby girl, and you can hang that ornament on our very first Christmas tree."

Instead he came to her and crushed her in a hug. "I am not sure what I ever did to deserve you, but thank you. For rocking my world. For loving me. And for giving me a second chance. I'm not going to let you down, Tori. Or our baby."

And when he'd hung the ornament on the tree, they stepped back, held hands and moved into a new future as a family.

* * * * *

*If you enjoyed this story,
look out for the next book in
South Shore Billionaires trilogy
Coming soon!*

*And check out these other great reads
from Donna Alward*

**Summer Escape with the Tycoon
Secret Millionaire for the Surrogate
Best Man for the Wedding Planner**

All available now!